what we were doing and where we were going

what we were doing and where we were going

Damion Searls

Dalkey Archive Press
Champaign and London

Library of Congress Cataloging-in-Publication Data

Searls, Damion.
What we were doing and where we were going / Damion Searls. -- 1st ed.
p. cm.
ISBN 978-1-56478-547-3 (pbk. : alk. paper)
I. Title.
PS3619.E2559W47 2009
813'.6--dc22
                              2008050050

Partially funded by a grant from the Illinois Arts Council, a state agency,
and by the University of Illinois at Urbana-Champaign

These stories were written in Oakland, Amsterdam, Cambridge (Mass.), and
Lisbon and Tours. The author is grateful to the Netherland America
Foundation–Fulbright Grant for support while in Amsterdam.
"A Guide to San Francisco" was published, in a slightly different form, in
Canteen magazine; special thanks to the editor, Sean Finney.
"56 Water Street" is for Danielle Searls.

www.dalkeyarchive.com

Cover: design by Danielle Dutton, illustration by Nicholas Motte
Printed on permanent/durable acid-free paper and bound in the
United States of America

Dedicated to Alan Searls

May 5, 1945 – December 19, 1980

Contents

Why does the painter need a model if he's going to deviate from it? I know the way Matisse laughs with his eyes, and when I put this question to him he laughed thus, silently. He told me, mischievously, that if there were no model one could not deviate from it. This seemed to me at the time a mere wisecrack. Then, as the years went by, the thing took its peculiar course within me: I began to love Matisse's very deviation from the model, the way he takes liberties with it. I understand him now, better than I understand myself.

Aragon, *Henri Matisse: A Novel*

56 Water Street

"I'll see you at five," my dear friend Simon Filigree said into the phone and hung up.

"Quiet," I said, "I'm writing."

"What is it?"

"A new book."

"Title?"

"*56 Water Street.*"

"Oh, about us." Simon was standing and I was sitting in the large sunny room that was my library, Simon's former den, and Lawrence Torrance's parlor in our house at 56 Water Street. The three of us had shared the house in college and for a few years more until Lawrence bought it. Now that Simon had moved out, Lawrence kindly let me stay indefinitely, rent-free, in a small attic room.

"Not exactly," I said. "We've had enough confessions."

"What's it about then?"

"Shall I tell you?" He sat down in Lawrence's leather armchair. "It is a watery book, sodden with the weight of the past. Like marshlands in the Austro-Hungarian Empire. But sparkly withal."

"In *Purgatory*," I went on, "near the beginning, Dante and Virgil have come up from Hell and walked down to the sea. The sun rises and:

> We were still beside the edge of the sea
>
> like people who are thinking about their journey
>
> who in their hearts go and their bodies stay.

They are 'like' exactly what they are. When the dead souls see that Dante is still alive they 'grow deathly pale'; his friend Casella asks why Dante is there and Dante says 'so that I may return here where I am making this journey.' *56 Water Street* is also about a man who circles back, who journeys to where he already is. I shall call him Casella. He is a fisherman in Italy, on the Tyrrhenian coast, it doesn't matter where. In Chapter One he mends his net, restoring the holes in the mesh to their proper places; in Chapter Two he repaints the hull of his little boat so that it looks the same as before; in Chapter Three he watches a storm at sea clear up as dusk falls, and the sky grows neither darker nor lighter."

"Sounds boring," he said.

"I hope so."

"Well let's hear some."

"That's all I have so far."

"What's all you have so far?"

"The title, *56 Water Street.*"

Simon stood up. "No one can ever understand what you're talking about," he said and left without another word. I turned back to my desk; the afternoon light made its way up the walls, yellowing with age. At precisely 6:15 I closed my notebook and stood up as well. It was time to go to Angela's for dinner.

Simon was just leaving with some sort of glare on his face when I arrived. "Remember what I said!" he said through clenched teeth. Angela and I embraced.

"I've already eaten," she said, "but I can make you something."

We sat down at the table together, and while I ate she described her day.

"And you?" she said.

"I have started a new book. Didn't Simon mention it?"

She looked down.

"*56 Water Street,*" I went on.

"What's it about?"

"Angela! You know I never like to talk about what I'm writing."

"But I so enjoy hearing you talk about it. Insight into the writer's mind at work and all."

I laid my hands on the table, palms up, in resignation.

"I hope it'll be longer than your last book?" she said.

I took out my small blue notebook. "Exactly this long. Or twice as long, but then I will have to order another."

"Ah, you brought it with you."

"Well I can't say no if you insist like that, after such a delicious dinner! It is about an Italian fisherman named Casella."

"Casella, that sounds like Angela. Is he based on me?"

"Not at all, it's from Dante. Now that you mention it, maybe I will put in a character named Angela, such a poetic name as I've always told you, but she will be nothing like you. I never copy real life."

Angela gulped down her wine.

"In the first chapter, Casella is mending his net. I shall have to research net-mending. I'll add that part later. Meanwhile he sees all sorts of debris on the beach: string like seaweed, seaweed like string. The castanet sound of the mussel shells . . ." My introduction had ended and the reading had begun. I pushed my chair back from the table, stared vacantly at a spot on the wall above Angela's head, and went on as listlessly as possible: "The trick is to catch the sea's gifts at the right moment. Casella has learned the lesson of water, which softens manmade stuff into natural beauty—driftwood, beach glass, sand—and eventually takes it all back again. The sea . . ."

"I don't like the word *stuff.*"

"Angela!"

"I'm just saying. The rest is poetic, it's nice, but 'manmade stuff'?"

I closed the notebook peevishly. "Well that's all I have so far." This wasn't strictly true, but if Angela was going to be like that about it. "He'll go fishing in Chapter Two."

"That's all there is in Chapter One? He mends a net and looks at some garbage?"

"Hmmph."

"Giles," she said after a long pause. "Why do you write these books of yours?"

It seemed like a fair question. After a moment I said, "So that I will have something I've written to read."

"Well no one else will read it! Simon told me your next book would be just like the last one."

"All Simon cares about when he reads is what happens next. If there's one thing in the world I'm not interested in, it's in what happens next!"

For some reason, this made Angela start to talk about us.

"Let's do something this weekend."

"Do something?"

"I don't know, anything. Can we take a drive out to the country?"

"Angela! But where? We haven't made plans, things might be closed, the weather. We don't know the best roads to take. One has to look into these things."

"You always say that and we never do anything. I want to take a drive out to the country this weekend!"

I made my excuses and plans for dinner the day after tomorrow, same time as today, then hurried home. A drive to the country this weekend—impossible. I reread what there was of *56 Water Street* and made a few minute corrections in blue pen until it was time for bed.

WEDNESDAY

At 10:15 sharp I woke up and consulted Aleksandr Sergeyevich Pushkin. Some people make lists or keep a diary, some read horoscopes or the I Ching, I consult a great Russian poet, with soulful eyes and enormous, expressive hands, one resting on a gold-tipped walking stick and the other at his side like a large friendly dog—too big for his body, like Michelangelo's David's. Pushkin always wears a severe black frock coat and a top hat, he is two feet high and made of painted wood, and today he looked quizzical, but stern. "Today," his face said, "you must avoid Simon, reflect on your friendship with Lawrence before meeting him for a drink this evening, go to the History of Science library to read *Spongien und Corallen des Adriatischen Meeres* volume II for *56 Water Street,* and remind Angela not to accept any invitations to parties, especially literary parties." I was so grateful to have Pushkin to guide me—all I ever wanted, really, from life was a mentor or director, someone's thumb I could trust and put myself under, and whose better than the great Russian poet's? I would have made a perfect little fascist, I thought. Except, I suppose, for all the killing and window-smashing.

I remembered a friend of Lawrence's who joined us once for a drink. He told us about all the degradations his boss put him through—humiliating meetings, taking credit for his ideas, publicly savaging the suggestions that his boss had forgotten were originally the boss's own—and then Lawrence's friend had said, "But I kind of like it." Lawrence, with his independent spirit, hadn't understood: "Well I wouldn't stand for it!" etc. But I understood perfectly.

Meanwhile a friend of mine had dropped by—"Away!" I cried, "I am writing!" for I couldn't very well tell Leo that I was preparing to reflect on my friendship with Lawrence. I had answered a phone call and several e-mails. The house made it hard to work, which was one of the things we had always liked about it. A stately Georgian affair, all pale plank facade and darkly harmonizing shutters, its pre-industrial architecture made it always pleasant inside, cool in summer and cozy in winter. Its tall first floor windows opened wide onto the quiet street between the university and the main café and bookstore area of town, so friends walked by and were in the habit of tapping on the glass if the windows were closed, or simply stepping through them into the living room if they were open.

Simon had had his eye on the place since the first week of freshman year, had cultivated the owner and was first in line when the older tenants moved out. The house went with his Oxbridge fantasies; if he could not live in a cramped stone chamber on the second floor (called the first floor in England) of a building named something like Chalmersby House, with a fireplace for heat and novelistic details on the mantelpiece (reproduction of a minor Jacques-Louis David engraving; 18th-century English fox-hunting watercolor, original), with dramas about trying to hide the tobacco smell of his pipe from the meddling housemaster—one could go on and on like this, the low armchair, grey rain against the small leaded-glass windowpane—if there were no such rooms or indeed civilization to be had in America, then Simon could at least receive callers in a large, high-ceilinged den, with several sofas for guests or new couples who found themselves here late at the end of a party, and a large strange painting that showed a boy in a white Shakespearean ruff on the footpath of what appeared to be a park in fin-de-siècle Vienna. Simon always said it was his great-grandfather Archibald Filigree as a boy, painted by his great-great-uncle Simon, for whom, at several Simons removed, he was named; in fact he had bought it at a yard sale and stored it for a year and a half before we moved in. His grandfathers were both named Bill. But Simon liked to entertain and he served his guests elaborate, old-fashioned cocktails and cucumber sandwiches. If he was, in short, born at the wrong place and time to attain Waugh or Forster or Powell, he could manage a sort of cross here between Scott Fitzgerald and Belle and Sebastian.

At the meandering rate of reflections and distractions like these, the morning was in danger of disappearing altogether. Yesterday, too, I had not exactly gotten cracking on Pushkin's instructions. So, without paying a moment's thought to Simon, I sat down at my desk to reflect on my friendship with Lawrence. In my files, under "L," were my previous reflections on Lawrence which I began by rereading:

1. A dear friend.

2. Very handsome. Blessed. Godlike. You make your offerings to him even though he is the last person in the world who needs them. He accepts them passively—strangely passive—maybe that's why we don't hold anything against him.

3. Business, busyness. Since last night at dinner he has hired his third permanent staff member, served a writ of injunction (which he tells me with great pleasure: "A writ!" he says, "of in-junc!-tion"), changed his tax status, restructured his website, dreamt up two new lines of business, replaced all the mouse pads in the office, and gotten his hair cut.

4. His father marries secretaries; current stepmother is younger than he (L.) is. Three brothers (no sisters) in their late 50s, titanically successful. Lawrence trying to find a new field, he

thinks so that he won't compete with his father and brothers but of course so that he can compete with a chance to do something they haven't done already. Huge strain under the langour.

Langour or frantic activity? The paradox of Lawrence.

5. Doesn't speak about himself; this is irritating sometimes. Is it false modesty? No. A way of keeping power over others; withholding; friendship on his terms.

After a moment's thought I wrote:

6. Generous to a fault. He scrambles to do favors, runs errands; listens for hours to other people's problems, gives advice, tries to solve their problems for them. Cf. #4, ¶2. So eager to go outside himself.

Not being able to accept a gift or take a compliment gracefully is so much less attractive than not caring about it at all. Why is that?

I took out my commonplace book and copied into Lawrence's file:

If any of us knew what we were doing, or where we are going, then when we think we best know! We do not know today whether we are busy or idle. In times when we thought ourselves indolent, we have afterwards discovered that much was accomplished and much was begun in us.

(Emerson)

Then, still later:

> 7. Lawrence has stayed my friend through it all. I am writing *56 Water Street* to honor him. ((To inoculate against Simon.))

It was now time for *Spongien und Corallen des Adriatischen Meeres,* volume II. It was a beautiful walk to the library, bright sun and a cool breeze, the treetops down by the river like a crowd at a parade, jostling for position, waving. I wondered if I was putting too many descriptions of the weather into *56 Water Street* and tried to notice people on the street instead: two thuggish teenage boys in baseball caps; my dear friend Georges, who stopped and told me all about the new book he was working on until I could finally get away; a woman with white hair and too-wide, staring eyes, whom I remembered from the bookstore trying to find some title without knowing the exact name of the book, the author, or the publisher, only that it had a pretty cover and was about "a marriage."

I was happier watching the weather, and by this point glad to get off the streets and step into the cool brick entrance hall of the History of Science library. The old wooden steps were there, shiny and slippery with decades or centuries of wear; the cast-iron handrail was sturdy and reassuring and I rested my hand at each landing on the cold iron sphere at the top of the rail. In the reading room a monument of Teutonic scholarship, just as solid and reassuring, was waiting for me behind the desk. Published in 1853 and probably unread since. Some of the large folio pages were still uncut, although someone had cut and looked at all the pages with tipped-in illustrations—hand-colored engravings of the corals of the Adriatic, or uncolored etchings of the coral-related devices and machines used down through the centuries. I read that the verb for obtaining corals was never clear, because of their ambiguous animal/vegetable status—did the Italian boys who could hold their breath the longest dive down to "gather" the corals or to "hunt" them? "catch" or "harvest"? I cut the pages which held nothing but botanical (or zoological) descriptions: measurements and facts and Linnaean Latin that I hunted or harvested. The feeling of knowledge gone quietly to waste—the hum of the air conditioners; the heavy, dark oak tables with their dim built-in brass lamps; carefully turning the tall, stiff pages, as if drying delicate porcelain plates with a handtowel—this was why I wanted to write *56 Water Street.*

By the end of the day the wind had picked up and I decided to stop by Angela's for a sweater before I met Lawrence. She was happy to see me and said so, for she had something to tell me:

"Don't forget to dress up tomorrow. After dinner we're going straight to Otto's party."

"A party?" I cried in dismay. "Otto?"

"It'll be fun. Your writer friends will be there, you know how Otto collects artist types."

"What an ass."

"Maybe we'll finally get to meet his wife."

"Ah yes, the mysterious . . . Sharka!" She was some kind of genius, always off studying the lesser potamogeton, whatever those were. (Insects? I wondered vaguely. Galaxies? Note: Look it up; maybe use in *56 Water Street.*) The research had turned lucrative and now they and their new baby were about to move out of university housing to a New York penthouse, Park Avenue even. Otto drizzled his time away at cafés or on stupid art projects in whatever medium attracted his narcissistic attention at the time; no one ever saw Sharka, but she seemed happy to support her older, tyrannical husband in sultanic style from behind the scenes.

Still brooding, I hurried across town but Lawrence was on time and there before me. I saw him walk back from the bar to our usual table where I had taken a seat. He was carrying two beers and the bartender's phone number. He set down the beers, took out his phone, and carefully programmed her number into it, then, scrupulously the gentleman as ever, he crossed out the number on the coaster until it was illegible, put the coaster face down, and put his beer on top of it.

"Lawrence! I was just reflecting on our friendship today. How are you?" He had left the house, as always, by the time I was up.

"Nothing special. You?"

"I have started writing a new book."

"A novel this time?"

"In a way. Well, more of a—hardly a—you could say so, but not really."

"I'd love to hear about it, but I know you say that disturbs your creative process."*

"It's about a fisherman, Casella. A sort of day-to-day account of his life." Lawrence never read my work, there was no point going into details.

"And how do you plan to make it appeal to the General Audience market?"

---

* He was always terribly polite.

With no answer to this rather staggering question, I sipped my beer in silence.

"How's Simon?" he said next.

"Simon?"

"When he moved out after Angela left him I thought I would be the one who stayed friends with him, but I never see him anymore, and I hear you hang out with him all the time."

I fell silent again. But Lawrence never seemed to care whether I answered his questions or not. He had an air of reciting them rather than asking them.

"Giles," he began again, "my father is coming to town on Friday and I don't want to see him alone. Can you join us for dinner?"

"Of course. Why is he coming?"

"He's getting another Lifetime Achievement Award on Sunday and coming early to see me."

"And your stepmother?"

"Leaving her at home this time. I don't think things are going well at the moment."

"Are you looking forward to seeing him?"

"Not really."** He hasn't said anything, but I'm sure he wants to visit the office, see how the business is growing. He'll have advice for me that I'd be stupid not to take, but I don't want to take any help from him. But I can't ignore his advice either, just to spite myself, that would be even weaker."

"Can't you take his advice and then forget it came from him, just give yourself credit for it? That's what I always do with my writing."

** An answer that direct was unusual. Lawrence must be under great strain.

"But deep down you know that it isn't yours."

"Do you?"

He seemed to take the question seriously and thought about it for some time, but kept the answer to himself, as usual.

"My middle brother is getting divorced too," he went on, as though this were continuing the subject of our earlier conversation along secret, subterranean lines. "Leaving Cheryl for a girl in Marketing. That's progress since the days of leaving your wife for a secretary, don't you think?"

"What does progress have to do with it?"

At this point, he made eye contact with a woman a few tables over, and she stood up from her boyfriend to go use the bathroom. Lawrence excused himself, went over, and asked her something with a shy smile while she waited in line. I slowly finished my beer and when Lawrence hadn't returned by then I went home.

THURSDAY

A day given over to *56 Water Street*. I had a difficult time not describing a particular shade of pink coral in the evening light as "incessant," but Georges had made that adjective his own. After dinner, lying idly on the sofa with my head propped up on my hand, I said to Angela:

"I'm not sure the pearls go with that green dress."

"Pearls go with everything," she informed me. "They make everything look better."

"Pearls are the new black?"

"Pearls are the old black."

Then we were on our way to the experimental university housing complex, cement block after cement block piled whimsically on top of each other, jutting out or up; window frames in bright white and rectilinear shapes in one strong primary color or another, like children's toys. I liked the buildings despite myself. Only whimsy is the antidote to concrete.

We went upstairs, a more complicated proposition than it might sound: each elevator went to different floors, or rather mezzanines, nothing more than corridors snaking around the building. Then there would be a half dozen steps up or down to another corridor, or a broadening out into a little foyer, like a meadow pool. Angela explained the advanced 1960s urban design ideas behind this arrangement while we walked and walked. In one little clearing we saw a group of Angolan boys playing soccer with a tennis ball; in another, a former professor of mine, doyen of medieval peasant studies, recently divorced and bankrupted in the process and living here now; finally we met someone with a guitar case who had just left Otto's party and could tell us the rest of the way.

When we arrived at last, a beautiful young woman opened the door with a radiant smile and told us where to leave our umbrellas. A second beautiful young woman holding a baby wafted past and offered to take our coats, and a third beautiful young woman emerged from the kitchen like a butterfly from a cocoon and asked what we wanted to drink. Angela and I were as if snow-blinded.

"Who are these people?" she whispered.

"I thought Sharka was supposed to be, um, rather ugly?"

"I know. And there're three."

"Is Sharka the one with the baby?"

"Then who's opening the door? who's pouring the drinks? and how come they all look like that?"

Complicated blended iced multicolored rum drinks in hand from #3, we went into the living room. It was a large bare room, hung only with Otto's unspeakable "surrealist" paintings and, above a small flat-screen TV, a floating shelf with a boxed set of Jean Cocteau's Orphic Trilogy and nothing else. A fourth exquisite nineteen-year-old was playing the acoustic guitar while she and a waifish boy sang—they looked like brother and sister, with the same impossibly upturned little noses, but they whispered to each other and kissed between songs, only adding to the atmosphere of decadence that surrounds extraordinarily beautiful people in any circumstances. Otto lay full length on the floor, wearing a stained gray hooded sweatshirt and sucking on the plastic-tipped end of the hood string. Otherwise the party seemed unremarkable.

I saw people I knew: Detlev, Didier, Georges of course, Népomucène. But Théophile, I knew from other parties, would have the information I wanted and would dispense it all to me, piece by piece like Pez, between sips of his drink. I seized the excuse to visit the kitchen's nymph again and brought Théophile a fresh glass, asking which one was Otto's wife. He knew who I meant. "Nannies," he said. Envy seethed in his voice.

"All of them?"

"Wants to be legal (a sip and a pause), pay taxes and everything (sip), not get caught later in his great career, wife's paying for it anyway. Students (big sip). Can't legally work more than 20 hours a week, needs a nanny 7 days, 8:30 in the morning to 10 at night, his great work you know, 94½ hours, five nannies, one's working now, paying one to tend bar, one to play music, the other's a guest, fifth couldn't make it."

His sixteen-sip glass was empty. I reported to Angela, who marched over to Otto and looked down at his infantile face, sucking the hood string.

"What's with the pornographic nannies?"

Otto took the plastic tip from his mouth and said slowly, mischievously, "pornographic?" Conversation around us stopped and Angela lowered her voice so that none of the nannies would hear.

"There's Pamela Anderson at the door" (it was true—streaked mountain of blonde hair, huge lips, huge breasts), "Barely Legal in the kitchen" (pony tail, tiny breasts, "Freshman Crew" t-shirt, braces), "Free Love on guitar, Dark And Stormy with the coats, all the archetypes. Who's number 5? Asian Spice? Fiery Redhead?"

A grin spread wider and wider across Otto's face; he even sat up on the floor; this was why he had invited her. He kept pornographic nannies in the first place not to sleep with them or even have them around to look at—he was too self-regarding for such pleasures— but to enjoy the reactions of the people around him, the audience at his court. Half his guests, if not more, were thinking it but Angela said it.

"You're just mad because I'm rich enough to hire them," he said slyly, inviting the next round. "That's my fault? I shouldn't give these girls jobs?"

"Where's your wife tonight?" Angela asked next, to let him know that she knew that it was his wife's money paying for all the nannies but that she would magnanimously forego the pleasure of rubbing that fact in his smug face. Both of them were thoroughly enjoying themselves now. I left them to their sparring.

"Giles!" It was Carruthers. "I hear you are writing a new book, always scribble scribble scribble eh what?"

"News travels fast."

"What is it then? More experimental whatnot?"

"No, it is *56 Water Street.*"

"Marmoreal title. Feels set in stone."

"Yes, well, it is about that. My hero, Casella, feels rather trapped."

"I hope it's not one of those books about someone stuck that never go anywhere? You know, 'My book isn't actually desperately dull, it's a vivid reflection of the ennui of modern life' and all that?"

"Oh it goes somewhere. All my writing is what has to get out of the way first—so you see, it goes—and then, when it's gone, I will be a new man who can write what comes next. It is like a preface. What's next is what matters."

"Didn't you say that last time?"

"Yes, it's what I always think."

"Quiet," I heard a voice say. "I'm writing."

In the corner was a pack of poets, each hunched over a scrap of paper making some sort of list. It turned out to be the Count To Ten game. Eduardo looked up first and declaimed, triumphantly:

"Whimper

Tutor

Traitor

Furor

Diver

Sinner
Cellar
Author
Never
Tenor."

As soon as he finished, Népomucène said, with satisfying crescendo:

"Anderson
Emerson
Ellison
Peterson
Paulson
Sexton
Stevenson
Orson
Donovan
Tennyson!"

This witty effort met with great acclaim. Kermit, the language poet, began to intone "Monastery, Catacomb, Circumambient," and we all lost interest.

"I'm with you, Giles," said Roland, returning to the earlier conversation. "I don't believe in change."

"How can you not believe in change?? Are you the same person you were in high school? Am I?" It was Hector, who had, it's true, as long as we'd known him, been a drab, sniveling sort but whose first book of poetry had won an award and who now ruled the roost.

Roland said: "In high school we were already the people who were going to turn into who we are to today. It's a matter of looking for continuities rather than discontinuities. You can always see the signs."

And in fact this retort made Hector fade drably back into the background.

"Yes, exactly!" I said. "Casella sets forth onto the trackless waters but always comes back home."

Ajax stepped in: "This perspective of yours is useless! It's all after the fact. At any given moment, what is someone supposed to do? 'Be himself'? Which self? 'Go with the flow'? Which flow?"

"I'm not giving anyone advice. I don't care what people do."

"You seem not to like it when anybody does anything!" cried Carruthers.

"On the contrary. I would like nothing more than to finish *56 Water Street*."

"What's the point???"

"I'll know when I finish."

At this moment of crisis in our debate I heard some sort of flourish from the other room and the door banged open: it was Otto, in white tights and an enormous papier-mâché mask, carrying a glass pitcher filled with a repulsive black liquid sludge. He had clearly been other than the center of attention for too long. Most ugly masks are moving and strangely beautiful in their way, but this was a gaping thing with splotchy eye sockets and colored circles on the cheeks that managed to be unredeemingly hideous.

"Behold!" someone murmured.

The beheld being, I learned, was Otto's newest project, an alter-ego of Jean Cocteau named John Cockwater. He went to the shelf and with flowing, balletic gestures took down the Orphic Trilogy and put a DVD in the player.

He flitted back into the other room for a moment and came out with a big cardboard box of masks, forcing one onto each of his guests. Some were handmade, others the cheap plastic Halloween kind: a pig, a Frankenstein, a Nixon, a hard plastic Power Ranger. On the TV a man fell through the mirror with a splash and was floating in a black void. I too lost track of time as the Cockwater events unfolded. At last Angela was back at my side, mask-free, and we hurried away. Outside it was raining again, but warmer; the fine rain only looked like snow as it slashed through the lamplight. We had been right to bring our umbrellas and wrong to leave them behind in our rush to escape but we were happy to be out in a world without performance art and in any case felt a need to be washed clean.

Angela took my upper arm and cuddled into my shoulder. "The party wasn't too awful, was it? Don't answer that. We need to do something to make it as though that party never happened, to bring us back to how we were before we ever saw those masks . . ."

When I got home I flung off my wet jacket and announced to Pushkin: "I have had a magnificent idea. On Saturday, I am taking Angela for a drive in the country!" His eyes widened in surprise.

FRIDAY

There were now preparations to make, routes to plan, picnic blankets to wash. I arose early, at 10, and tried to accomplish as much as I could before lunch

Angela and I had decided to make an event of it and rent a BMW convertible. When I was at the car rental agency, looking at their laminated sheet (I love laminated sheets), I remembered the chance of rain, and thought what if we can't get the top closed in time, and thought another Leisure Class car would be just as nice. Then I thought that without a convertible we didn't need all that space . . . I ended up with a Ford minicompact, I was sure Angela wouldn't mind the change in our plans. It is I who do not like to change plans.

Soon I was hurrying home to try to squeeze in an afternoon of work on *56 Water Street* before it was time for dinner with Lawrence and his father. I felt the book nearing its conclusion but the question was how Casella's story should end. And alongside that question, another: what *was* his story? I had realized, sometime after I decided to take Angela on a drive to the country, that Dante's own story is not nearly as static as Casella's or that of the souls turning deathly pale; they are all fixed but Dante moves, and the return he longs for takes place only after the narrative ends. I wondered if Casella's story as I had imagined it might not, after all, be the least little bit too boring? Should something happen?

As I walked in the door, Simon stood up from Lawrence's leather armchair. His costumes had gotten more and more insistent over the years, more overdetermined around a theme to make sure that people picked up on it: today he was wearing a tweed jacket with brown leather elbow patches over a polo shirt, and tan riding pants tucked into his calf-high boots.

After short, warm greetings he began:

"It's not right what you're doing to Angela."

Here it was, an inner conversation I had had with myself for years seeing the light of day at last. Simon and Angela seemed to be a perfect couple back in college—outgoing, comfortable enough with each other to be friendly with everyone else, a well-oiled team. Angela liked Simon's fantasy worlds, whether Oxbridge or great-great-uncle Simon or the Roaring Twenties with gin fizzes, and if he never paid much attention to Angela's inner world then perhaps it was better that way. A certain outwardness, in them both, was what made them seem "perfect" because no couple's inner world, good or bad, is ever understood by anyone else; what we call perfect couples are simply those with a good public presence. He threw parties, she made canapes and got drunk and danced, and if she sometimes cornered a guest to complain bitterly and euphemistically of her unhappinesses, was this really much more than a touch of later Fitzgerald, a smudge of chiaroscuro? Are we ever truly unhappy, then when we think we best know our sad hearts? In every situation we find ourselves in, have we not chosen the set of confrontations and miseries we feel most comfortable with, which most become us?

When Angela left Simon there was an ugly scene, with harsh words whose delicate details were wisely kept from me but whose gist was clear enough. What kind of life was Angela going to have with me now? I spent months waiting for this demand to be made to my face, harsh words and all, but I came to realize, as I settled into the new state of things with Angela, that Simon was the last person to bring up such questions. He shrank away from introspection or psychology—individual identity was expressed, for him, through style, and even how you behaved showed your style, which code you chose to follow and which role you had decided to play. Nothing about the inner life. His own life continued on much the same lines after leaving 56 Water Street; the house decor went back into storage and out came the furnishings for an apartment a few blocks away, the locale for his fantasy hero's next chapter: a small London flat, cool water seeping through the wallpaper, heavy brown sideboard, the landlady's lace doilies as the object of dry narratorial witticisms. Drab, postwar food-rationing parties, with grey suits and tins of beans.

I wondered what sort of crisis Simon must be undergoing for all this to come out in the open now.

"?—"

"She needs to go out and enjoy life, not be stuck at home having dreary dinners, only getting to go to the parties she drags you to. She deserves better. Someone who appreciates the finer things. She's been trying to get you to go on a drive out to the country for months and all you do is make excuses."

"But, Simon, we are going tomorrow!"

He looked startled, but skipped ahead in the speech he had mentally prepared. Once one starts these things one can't change course, one has to carry them through to the end.

"When is the last time you took her out to a restaurant with a decent wine list? Or even to a movie? With a plot," he added quickly.

"Angela can do whatever she wants with her time. And—But—Simon, what are you trying to tell me?"

"She shouldn't be stuck with you!" he said through clenched teeth once again.

"I don't doubt that you're right. But I'm not holding her prisoner. She is doing what she wants."

Such a simple fact was hard to deny. Simon sputtered a bit and was gone, and with a quick glance at Pushkin, whose sardonic eyes gave me just the sympathy I needed, I sat down at my desk.

Ah, Casella! You too are doing what you want. Who am I to force you into more of a story, away from your nets and your round window overlooking the storms of the Tyrrhenian Sea? I returned to my humble tasks until it was time to meet Lawrence and his father for dinner.

Mr. Torrance had thick hair, bright white small teeth, and a firm handshake. "Giles, good to see you again. Still writing? Since graduation? Larry tells me you've started a new book."

I had never heard anyone call Lawrence "Larry" but I was physically unable to turn and look or even glance at him to see his reaction. The pull of his father's smile was too strong.

"He's told me about you too, sir. Congratulations on your latest Award."

"Never mind that. What are you drinking?"

Lawrence's habitual silence took on new shades of meaning as he watched his father charm me. It was Lawrence's way of disdaining to compete without seeming sullen; he gave off an air of the whole thing taking place under his own auspices.

Soon, having decided I was firmly in his pocket, Mr. Torrance turned his attention back to his Larry.

"How's Mom?" Lawrence slipped in before his father could start.

"Oh, she's fine, minding the garden. How's busin—"

"And Gary and Cheryl?"

Lawrence's father refused to be put off balance. The drinks arrived, giving him time to regroup, propose a toast to "Old friends" (winking at me), and start a long, impressive story about a company of whose ground floor Gary's venture capital firm had got in on.

It went on like that for a while, my head turning from side to side as I followed their long baseline volleys. I saw why Lawrence had wanted me to come but it didn't seem to be working, both the Torrances were ignoring me. Then again, who knows how it would have been without me?

I had drifted off into my own thoughts, and the drinks which kept coming were stronger than bartenders were wont to make when I ordered them, when I saw Lawrence's father standing a few tables over; Lawrence and I found ourselves getting up to follow him.

"Now what are you two lovely ladies doing sitting here all by yourself?" Lawrence's father was saying.

A look of intense pain passed across Lawrence's face, but the women in question smiled. Lawrence's father went on: "I'm in town to see my boy here." When the women turned to appreciate Lawrence their smiles grew warmer, but then they did turn back to his father, smiles' added warmth intact.

We sat down.

Before too long Mr. Torrance had ordered a round of drinks for the table, handing his black American Express card to the waiter and making sure we noticed, and before too much longer I was saying "Lawrence's father is the guy who came up with the idea to flash the temperature along with the time on those signs outside banks!"

"Really??"

"Yes, well," he began smoothly, "we knew that the time is what everyone wants to see, but the backers needed to make your eyes linger, stray to their logo and remember it. With just a clock you would glance at the time and then that would be that."

"But I love it when I see the temperature on those signs! I don't need to know the temperature, I already know how it feels outside, but it's always such a bonus!" One of the ladies filled the pause Mr. Torrance had infinitesimally inserted.

"You see?" he smiled.

"He even patented it!" I added. I seemed to be playing the same role opposite Lawrence's father as I had so often with Lawrence: the sidekick, the straight man. But it was a relief to have any part to play at all, after the long family duel or duet I had witnessed, and somehow even being a sidekick felt like partaking in Lawrence's father's glory.

"Registered intellectual property," he corrected modestly.

It was utterly tacky of me to continue, but I willingly offered up my dignity. One starts these things and one has to carry them through to the end. Besides, I do love this story. "That means every time the temperature is displayed on any of those signs, anywhere in the world, he gets paid 1/25 of a cent. It adds up!" I felt like a pimp. I was almost leering.

He smiled again, even more charmingly, and the lovely lady who hadn't spoken dropped something and bent down to pick it up, adjusting her chair at the table and accidentally brushing her thigh against his, without seeming to notice. She left it there. Within half an hour Lawrence's father had left with both, abandoning Lawrence to me and the Oedipal resentment simmering within him. I was not surprised to be returning home alone a short while later. In any case, I needed a good night's sleep—tomorrow I was taking a drive to the country!

FIVE — OUR DRIVE IN THE COUNTRY

(Short notes; one must live in the present on days like this)

The river is shrouded in a hazy afternoon sunlight, even though it is morning. Gnats or dust drowsing through the air. We see an egret.

"Angela, I feel that last night with the Torrances will change *56 Water Street*. Casella remains where he is, but how did he get there? What inheritance brought him to his place? What does it mean that a family line is traditionally called a 'house'? What *is* 56 Water Street?"

"You must have been thinking about that all along—the whole book is called *56 Water Street*."

"But I never knew why."

We see a great blue heron, alone, standing in the marsh. Slowly, deliberately, it takes off. A coat tossed onto a coat rack, limp and loose, become a gray sail, swelling with the wind.

Sun dapples onto us from two directions at once: down through the trees, up from the river.

Angela: "Are you going to write an occasional poem?"

"Are Casella's parents in the book?"

"No!" I cried. "As a writer you have to simplify things. Be centripetal. In life itself there is Lawrence, his father, his stepmothers, the brothers Gary, Barry, and Harry, everyone has their problems and their own inner nature, I can't go down all those side roads. I feel differently about them all and the trick is to condense all those feelings into my emotions for a single character, Casella—that is what gives the book a center."

"So Casella is your friend Lawrence?"

"I never copy real life."

Walking through the forest. As always, it's disappointing to have to look down the whole time so as not to lose my footing on the path. Today I remember to stop and look up more than usual.

"Is Casella married?"

"He lives alone. A real fisherman would be married but he is supposed to be a still character, stable, content, and other people change you, drive you forward."

"You never understand what I'm talking about!"

"What? The hero, Casella. I was just telling you that I should have him redecorate his house, maybe buy a new tablecloth that looks like . . ."

"How long have we been together, Giles?"

"Let's see. You were with Simon since junior year, then you and I ran into each other when we were traveling—"

"Two and a half years!"

"Yes, that sounds right."

"I know!"

Our conversation seemed to be drifting farther and faster than ever.

"Giles, don't you wish we could just keep driving?"

"Driving where?"

"I don't know, but it's so hard to leave the city, you have to fling yourself out, almost desperately, and now that we have it seems a shame to turn back. We could just keep going. I feel like it's our last chance."

"For what?"

"For something, I don't know what."

"But Angela, you don't really believe that. You'd miss your home, friends, your collection of gourmet vinegars. Even if there were something you wanted to escape from, we don't believe it's possible to escape, now do we?"

"Fine. Let's go back."

"But—"

"No, I've decided."

Night falls on the drive home. We merge into the rotaries too fast, grip the steering wheel too tight.

SIX

This morning Pushkin's face was cold and implacable, even for a Sunday. His hand loomed ominously at his side like a Biblical prophet's. "You must come to an understanding," his face said, "of the events of the past two days. There are powerful currents beneath the surface of things," Pushkin added, "and it is a time of great importance, but also danger, for you." I was surprised at his grave, oracular tone but immediately felt what he said to be right. I called Angela to see if I could come over earlier than planned, but she wasn't at home. Strange.

Everything had to do, I thought, with the house. I looked around my attic room, long and thin, which I had divided into two areas but with no door between them. The roofs sloped on the the front of the house and more steeply on the two sides. A low bed, a small table, a hard chair. I liked it that way, and did not want to live downstairs again in the high-ceilinged rooms with soft furniture, but maybe Simon was right, two and a half years ago, to leave. Should I, too, abandon 56 Water Street?

The doorbell rang; only mailmen didn't knock on the window, so I went downstairs. I was almost to the bottom when I remembered it was Sunday. It was a courier service, with a large package; I asked if I could sign for Lawrence, but it was for me.

Inside an oversized yellow envelope were two short notes folded in half, on the same stationery, and two large bundles rubber-banded together:

"Dear Giles,

I am leaving with Lawrence for Buenos Aires. Please don't try to follow us (ha!) I'm giving you back all our pictures and the poems you wrote for me. Good luck with your writing. Goodbye forever.

Love, Angela"

"Giles,

Angela and I are off. No hard feelings I hope. I can't sell the house for tax reasons, so it's yours to keep; enclosed herewith are the title and the necessary documents. Don't forget to talk to a lawyer about the inheritance tax.

Yours ever, L."

∎

I moved into Larry's rooms. Some time later, Simon surprised both himself and me by moving back into his old rooms at 56 Water Street, which I offered him rent-free. He thought, as Lawrence had, that the falling out with me over Angela was what had torn him away from the house but for some reason with Lawrence gone Simon was happy to move in again. He hung Archibald Filigree back on the north wall, resumed throwing his Twenties parties, and I was happy to have him back.

∎

"I'll see you at five," my dear friend Simon said on his way out to a badminton tournament.

"Quiet," I said, "I'm writing."

"What is it?"

"A new book."

"Title?"

"From Emerson: *What We Were Doing and Where We Were Going.*"

"What's it about?"

"Shall I tell you?"

The Cubicles

It is a little strange that—although I think of myself as a writer who responds, describes, rereads and rewrites, not as a writer with something inside himself that he tries to "express"—an autobiographical impulse should once again have taken possession of me, after my two years in the cubicles, and that I should want to set down my real-most self in precisely the period when that self was least real. The most intense (if that is the right word) of my experiences there in the cubicles was the lack of experience, the timelessness and stasis: in any job, you sell the employer your time, but among the cubicles you never get it back. Even the physical space of the cubicles was a sort of allegory of the isolated compartments in which your hours find themselves there, like cabinets in a tea shop, hundreds of square drawers taking up the whole wall, each one with barely enough room on the front for a knob and a number or a Chinese character, each one smothering a wonderful scent in its conformity. One of those cubical drawers holds what you want, the new sensation you desperately need to awaken you from your present stagnation, but which? There are no interactions among the cubicles, encounters which might change you, move you forward; I learned to my cost and dismay that the exaggerated paranoia about coworkers in the corporate world is only too justified, and once you recognize this fact and act accordingly all that's left of human interaction are isolated incidents. Work is the negation of plot, of story, though the incidents there do illuminate character; what I have to tell about my years in the cubicles is therefore not a narrative, but at best a thin little tale like Hawthorne's tales, or a tale like Chaucer's, worthy (if at all) only to while away an empty hour by describing a possibly unfamiliar mode of life and some of the individuals who move in it, among whom the author managed to be one for a time.

■

In a small town in northern California, at the edge of what, in the days of old Ralston and Hearst, was a vibrant agricultural valley— some of the best farmland in the country even a century ago, even after the Crystal Springs Dam turned San Andreas Valley into the bottom of a reservoir in order to raise land values in San Francisco and make possible prestigious manor lawns and an English-style park which Frederick Law Olmsted refused to design on the utterly unsuitable sand dunes to the west of the city—at the edge of this valley, now burdened with industrial parks and overcrowded freeways and little but symptoms of a so-called service economy, except for some retail chain stores whose low-paid employees cannot afford to live anywhere nearby—here, gleaming in the sunlight which now seems artificial too, stand shining cylinders of glass and steel, with a grand view of all there is to see, mainly each other. These buildings, beautiful in their strident, unnatural way, along with a dozen or so nondescript buildings nearby, are the home—they call it the "campus"—of the corporation whose name is wrapped around the top of the highest cylinder, the corporation which I will call Prophet Corp., pun intended. Who knows what subliminal effects it had on us to say to ourselves "Profit . . . Profit . . . Profit" every time we saw the company name up there like the morning star, or crouching in monumental stone throughout the "campus," or glittering on our ID cards and screen savers and free ballpoint pens?

The glass and steel cylinders—these were called "The Towers"—crowd around one of several artificial lakes left over from the previous tenant, a marine theme park. Along with the lagoons, complete with geyser-like fountains, are leftover sea fowl—herons, egrets, swans, numerous species of migrating ducks and geese and gulls—who spend most of their time looking baffled, huddling at the edge of a now urbanized pond or shepherding their children across paved roads whizzing with cars and SUVs. Whether the disoriented birds appreciate it or not, the landscaping here is superb, in corporate America's typical Impressivist style along with a few faux-Japanese gardens and slate fountains as a nod to one of the several hobbies, not to say fetishes, of Prophet Corp.'s autocratic yet jaunty leader. Bustling through this landscape—perhaps to one of the excellent restaurants masquerading as cafeterias in the various Towers, each specializing in a different international cuisine; or perhaps to the private campus gym; or leaving or arriving at work, for in the abstract new world of Prophet Corp. regular hours are by no means necessary, and in fact seem thoroughly out of date—briskly striding around the lagoon, looking in no way baffled whatsoever, you might at any time have seen polished marketing women, in their regulation thick inch-and-a-half black heels, dashing off to impress a new client or go to the gym or go "partying" in the city, certainly not dashing home or into their offices. Here too you might have seen small groups of engineers or programmers, in jeans and sneakers or khakis and chambray button-down shirts with *Prophet* embroidered on the breast pocket, chatting among themselves in Hindi or Tamil or Ukrainian. Likewise the managers, slightly better dressed, walking always alone, looking regal and carefree or careworn and anxious according to the latest numbers.

Taken together, these individuals sometimes made the campus a stirring scene. But enter one of the buildings—mine was Prophet Plaza, for straight is the gate and narrow the way to an office in The Towers—hold your ID card to the door sensor, either by hunching your shoulders and doubling over or by raising one hip in a crippled twisting leap (some wear their badge clipped to breast pocket or lapel, others on their belt); climb a flight or two of stairs for the day's physical exercise, or take a short elevator ride, and repeat the dance of the badge on your floor; enter, and you will sense, not see, what lies backstage behind the bustle: row upon row of seated figures, in ergonomic chairs to discourage lawsuits. Some are working; more are pretending to work, or checking their e-mail, or simply sitting in that stupor of passing the time which is far more exhausting than all but the hardest labor. An unlucky few are seated near the door, their presence or absence revealed to all who enter; distracted every time the door slams, for who in the internet age has time to shut a door softly behind oneself; and, because bad luck always comes in threes, these same unfortunates are the ones who have to get up and open the door whenever someone forgets their high-security badge and pounds to get in. Pass through this purgatory as quickly as you can, along corridors of dull gray lined with openings at regular intervals and dotted between the openings with Dilbert and Far Side cartoons and sailboat or puppy dog calendars and the occasional art postcard (Toulouse-Lautrec's *Chat Noir* is a perennial favorite), make your way on the C wing of the second floor of Prophet Plaza to cubicle C02– –, and there, dear reader, not long ago, you might have recognized the author of these pages, or a cryptic "W@H" on his eraserboard to tell you that he was "Working at Home." Today you would seek him in vain; a worthier successor wears his dignity, uses his password, and lives in a part of the world where the wages are but a fraction of what Prophet has to pay its employees here.

For times have changed once more in this valley in northern California. When I first arrived in my cubicle, I found a Welcome Kit with a free license-plate frame announcing "PROPHET: The Internet *Changes* Everything"; "*Changes*" was even in red as well as italics, like the words of Jesus in bedside Bibles, for so ran the new gospel, and to this day I do not know the extent to which I believe in it. Some time before, at the height of the internet boom, the jaunty yet autocratic leader I have already mentioned decreed that the "e" in "Prophet" should become italic, and it did not seem worthwhile to go back and make the name consistent: as at the birth of our Savior, a new era had begun, and you can now see at a glance whether an entryway sign or monument in stone or ID card dates from the new dispensation or the barbaric, pagan past. That sly little *e* assures all and sundry that Proph*e*t truly does herald a new world, smooth and curvy and sexy like the *e* which hurries toward it, leaning into the headwind blowing from paradise. Or so it seemed in the handful of years before March or April or September 2001. The Christian Era, a leisurely 2,000 years in icthyic Pisces before moving on to the Age of Aquarius, proved no suitable model after all for this fast-paced new era. Now that same *e* symbolizes the green world of future itself hurrying away from the few people left scrambling to catch up to its sheltering riches.

I noticed such things as italicized and unitalicized "*e*"s because I was at Proph*e*t Corp. as an editor, of training materials in the division of Education—later eLearning, still later *i*Platform—Services. (Not a soul I spoke to could tell me what "*i*Platform" is supposed to mean; "*i*" usually stood for "internet" when I was there, but that does not get one very far.) All in all, the last year of the boom and my first in the cubicles was an excellent year for vowels, and a bad year for parts of speech: VPs discussed "rearchitecting the enterprise to take on a more consultative role"; rising corporate stars described, somewhat vaguely, how they planned to "incent sales team members to uplift the cross-sells and downlift the losts." Nouns were the hardest hit, as address books became Contact Management Solutions and useless old manuals were born again as "legacy courseware." But was this really so different from graduate school, which I had left and whose debts I was still paying off? There, books were "technologies of affect production" and authors, or "author-functions," were sites of cultural practice; at least here there was someone to tell me that yes, it *did* make a difference, we would *make more money* if only we wrote that our products "empowered the end-user" or "gave a 360 Degree View of the customer 24x7." In truth, alas, no one ever did tell me that, not literally, and yet everyone acted as though someone in Marketing had announced something to that effect, and surely this Someone In Marketing must have concrete information somewhere to prove it—a study in some business journal, maybe a focus group. Where else could this terrible jargon have come from? I daydreamed about updating Orwell's classic "Politics and the English Language" as "Business and the English Language," but not for long; like my other former-intellectual colleagues in the Editorial Group, I soon learned to ignore Strunk & White as a legacy prose management solution and simply capitalize the buzzwords as ordered. Why on earth not?

It was a wonderful humanistic bubble, the Editorial Group, airy and carefree under the badly applied wallpaper of Prophet's corporate culture. The higher-ups had finally been convinced that, for some incomprehensible reason, you had to take perfectly good documents which someone had already written and show them to someone else—worse, a refractory hairsplitter who cared more about pointless details such as grammar than about the product's Time To Market. Having been convinced, they more or less threw up their hands and left us to perform our arcane rituals as we saw fit. My direct supervisor, who set the daily workload quotas and defined how our tasks were scheduled, was a former editor herself—her many predecessors having been promoted to their own levels of incompetence—and thus on our side; our only audience was the engineers whose work we were editing, who couldn't write in the first place, and we played to that audience perfectly. Never once in my years at Prophet did a word of feedback penetrate back through the marble silence of the cubicles, whether from management or the semi-mythical customers who were said to have to read the incommodities we produced. (I say "semi-" because I once saw such a beast, on a plane reading one of our textbooks. He told me that no one could ever understand them, including the instructors who had to teach from them.)

In short, our crew of haggard graduate students, traumatized museum employees, pulverized teachers, resigned to relative poverty in the service of culture—gardening for turnips as it were in the middle of the Gold Rush—had, each of us, somehow found a secret door low in the wall, had opened it and been transported to the green and gentle slopes of Arcadia, where there was little work to do, even less supervision, and a corporate mandate not to waste time doing that little work well. Most days we telecommuted—a euphemism for checking our e-mail and voice mail once or twice, to make sure that nothing came up, as in fact it always did. Two or three of our number, I was told, etherealized into some still higher circle of paradise, never dreamed of making their appearance at the cubicles which stoically bore their names; their disembodied voices phoned into weekly meetings, and once or twice a year, perhaps on their Saint's Day or lured by the extravagant catering of our more supposedly important corporate events, they would descend to campus, go carelessly about what they called their duties, and, at their own convenience, rise once more into the empyrean.

Mindful of the parable of the workers in the field, with lightsome hearts and the happy consciousness of being usefully employed—in our own behalf, at least—we went through the various formalities of office without a splinter of envy for these corporate cherubim. Scrupulously did the Ph.D. in English capitalize the first word of each and every sentence! Thunderingly did the art historian insist on changing double-hyphens to dashes, and politely refrain from pointing out that Chapter 3 was clearly taken from the wrong book! To the death did we struggle in meetings over whether to write "e-business," "E-business," or "*e*Business"! Those meetings were an elaborate tissue of the standards we pretended to have, the care we pretended to take, and the work we pretended to do—a sort of Noh play of productivity.

I soon grew to like all my colleagues. Most of them had some good traits, and our life of ease and a fantastic stock purchase plan brought out those qualities in them and an open-minded goodwill in me. It was pleasant, after leaving home at 11 in order to miss the commute, to speed down the usually clogged highways, across the Bay Bridge with the Golden Gate and Marin and Mt. Tamalpais shining in the midday sun or looming in the San Francisco fog; pleasant to arrive at my cubicle, check my e-mail, add a few desultory periods to the ends of sentences, and feel the hum of similar activity coming from whichever one or two nearby cubicles were occupied today. A long and pleasant lunch downstairs, perhaps with today's officemate; some more work before leaving by 2, or at the latest 3, to miss the commute—so passed day after day, month after month, in sunny stillness.

It would be a sad injustice to portray everyone at Prophet as leading this life of Circean pleasures. Outside our group, there were men and women of vigor and ability, working long, hard hours with an energy altogether superior to the cause which their unlucky stars had destined them to serve. One man in particular, in the Publishing Group closely connected with our Editorial Group, possessed truly exceptional gifts: he was diligent, prompt, kind, acute, actually trained and experienced in the line of work where he now found himself and thus knowledgeable to an extent which would have put the rest of us to shame if we had had any. Difficulties and intricacies, large and small, which presented themselves to his attention soon lifted like morning mist in the clear light of day; he had mentored all the publishers, all the editors too, and stood in my mind as both the ideal of his type and the real mainspring which kept our whole operation moving. It was a sad day—the very same day that I edited a new mandatory training course for Prophet managers, on "Managing Talent": how talent is *potential* as well as *performance*; how crucial it is "in this new economic climate" to use the Talent Grid (potential on one axis, performance on the other) to evaluate employees and make sure you "have the *right person* in the *right job* at the *right time*"—it was a sad Friday morning at the end of the month when he showed up at work to a voice-mail message telling him that this day was to be his last. No doubt he had a slightly higher salary than the rest of us and was thus the best cost to cut. How convenient his cubicle proved itself then! Nail a board on the top and another over the entrance and there is your coffin, the still-warm body already inside.

I must confess that a rib of integrity or editorial principle occasionally revealed itself under my colleagues' soft flesh, or even my own. On the whole, however, it would be no slander to characterize the Editorial Group as a pack of carpet-bagging wretches, who abandoned everything worth preserving from our varied life experiences and brought to our cubicles the merest specter of our humanity. Between us, we had lived decades in Italy and France and Germany and England and India and Japan, written novels and dissertations and books of poetry, lived centuries of active life with youthful wonder before putting ourselves out to pasture and all but vanishing. In one way or another, we all disappeared in or into our cubicles.

One of the editors was the most birdlike individual I have ever met—more in the wren or chickadee line than crow or goshawk, needless to say. A late addition to our group, hired to fill out our "head count"—it was corporate policy to reward the wasteful and penalize the thrifty: if a group could get by for a month or two understaffed, they would never get their full allotment again—she fulfilled this requirement to perfection. It took her a long time to do much of anything in the way of actual editing, but she excelled at gathering post-it stickies in a wide range of colors and building an elaborate nest on the margins of the document for her brood of queries and uncertainties. This nest seemed to be her sole concern; she imperceptibly resolved her questions, watched the stickies fly off, and left the unchanged document none the wiser. She was unnaturally small and thin, preternaturally retiring and soft-spoken on the rare occasions when she spoke at all, and even rarer were the occasions when I saw her dart down the corridors; most often I saw her perched in her cubicle or simply found that she had alighted at our meetings, with the same portion of bagels or donuts or fruit before her as the rest of us, and practically the same portion at the end of the meeting too, after an hour or two of pecking at it.

To comprehend and portray a character under such difficult circumstances would require the long contemplation and lightning single stroke of a Japanese brush painter. Here and there, pausing in midflight to sip a tiny drop of nectar from a fuchsia or morning glory, she let me perceive for a moment a fascinating figure, who had spent years living in Asia, had left a husband and two children for a passionate new midlife love affair; whose older daughter had fallen in with a vagabond hippie drug dealer, given birth to a granddaughter and named her Starlight, or Symphony, I don't quite recall. But what color is the hummingbird's chest if it is red in one light, blue in another, and green from a third angle? I can imagine an inner life which combines the fleeting movements I saw with the concrete facts I heard—her spirit, I imagine, was characterized throughout by a certain uneasy activity, which she gratefully anchored in the quicksand of difficult but stable situations; when the moment came, I would guess it took no great burst of strength to break her bonds, she could simply slip through the mesh of the net and be off; her time in the cubicles, I conceive, was just another self-imposed period of relative rest—but all of this is fiction. In the realm of fact, the domain of this tale, her portrait in my gallery of cubicle dwellers must remain a monochrome, gestural sketch.

My other colleagues I can describe more solidly. One editor, a thin, pale woman of nunlike propriety, seemed to fasten onto her spirit the front door which our cubicles lacked. She glared at us with the fixed, suspicious stare that we all adopt when peering through a peephole to see who is at the door; even her gestures of kindness seemed furtive, slipped out to us like a secret note between schoolgirls or something smuggled into a prisoner's jail cell. My similes drift, I notice, between passing something in and out and around, but she was like that, an entangler of prepositions, a one-way mirror. I found her remarkably difficult to talk to, as she was too suspicious to answer the most trivial of questions without first investigating the terrain and making sure that the question was not some sort of trap. "Is 'connectivity' jargon, or should I leave it?" "How do *you* feel about it?"—"Are you heading home?" "Why do you ask?" No one else seemed to notice this trait, or mind it; perhaps they never asked any questions. In me the sheer perfection (sheer like a cliff) of her inscrutable façade inspired a sort of faith in the intelligence which surely must lie behind it. I thus admired her even before the incident I hinted at earlier, which I may not have the space to discuss in more detail—the one which taught me the value of absolute privacy and impersonality among the cubicles. Afterwards I saw this impenetrable colleague of mine as wise indeed.

Still later, my admiration changed to wonder. A preponderance of gay men and partnered straight women more or less eliminated the terror of sexual harassment lawsuits in my group, and we were able, to a greater extent than in most American corporations, if not to discuss any details then at least to acknowledge that sexuality exists in the world. Not so my nunlike colleague of the long, severe dresses; there was nothing in particular that she said to express discomfort, but much, indeed everything, that she didn't say, and her high, thin gaze would sweep down from above her crucifix necklace or pearls like a frigid Arctic wind to cool anyone's faintest interest in mentioning such matters around her. She was married and, not having met the blushing bridegroom, I felt vaguely sorry for him, although I'm sure their house was kept lovely. Then I learned of her wild years: sleeping with uncounted classmates and teachers in the

States, and then bringing a series of criminals back to her room for the night, one after another, from the streets of the Eastern European university town where she was studying. These stories were not from the most reliable source, and were, I am sure, exaggerated, but they could not have been wholly fabricated; after hearing them, I used to watch and study her with, I think, livelier curiosity than any other form of humanity presented to my notice at Prophet Corp. Her bifurcation was either spatial or temporal: what one must assume is a significant part of her life existed either at home but not here, or in the past but not now, and either way her powers of auto-amputation were cause for astonishment. I watched, I studied, but my conclusions went no further than that her adaptation to our form of life, whether a product of will or damage, was perfect. It might be difficult—it was difficult—to imagine the shape and tone of the rest of her life, but of everyone I have ever known, she was the fittest to find a place among the cubicles.

There were, as I have said, members of our group whose seniority had almost completely absolved them of material presence; among the rest, the most venerable was the man who had first found the secret door low in the wall, and had brought so many after him. More than half our number had been recruited by him or were his grandchildren, so to speak: recruits of his recruits. He was firmly established as the beloved head of an Arcadian dynasty—unlike Moses, he too had reached the promised land—and even those such as myself who were not his descendants could not help but see him as a kindly grandfather: gentle, generous, tinged with the patina of an earlier time. He had been working at Prophet (only later at Prophet) for four years when I started, an almost unheard-of span among the cubicles. He was the editor I became closest friends with, or closest to friends with; I also saw him the least, because he started his days in the cubicles at 5 or 6 A.M., like a living embodiment of some ancestral anecdote about walking miles to school every day, through the snow. Only on his busiest days did he stay at the office until I arrived. We talked about movies, but never saw any together; he had been writing a dissertation too, on Nathaniel Hawthorne, ten or twenty-five years ago, and once thought of writing novels; now these and all his other projects did nothing but sun themselves on the sandy shores of someday, and his extracubicular activities— the movies he did see, the annual trip to a classical music festival abroad—had taken on the faintly depressing whiff of "hobbies."

Such were some of the people with whom I now found myself connected, or at least the shapes to which I now found myself adjacent, for it was only in the editor of cubicle C02-- that I could perceive a full person, most of whose capacities remained off-campus insofar as they remained at all. Literature, its exertions and objects, took on a new tone in my life: I read, but barely wrote, and then only vaporous, repetitive ambiences which I convinced myself were poems; my diary became little more than a book of quotations copied from what I read; I told myself that this was a good year, and then a good two years, to be receptive and absorbent, after the long—and not, in any case, rewarding—labors of graduate school. A gift, a faculty, if it had not departed, was suspended and inanimate within me.

In one form or another, this same change, or syndrome, came over everyone among the cubicles: I mean a certain loss, in an extent proportional to the strength or weakness of one's character, of the self-generative mobility which distinguishes us from the vegetable kingdom. The fable of the Devil's wages, gold which saps those it enriches, was as applicable here as elsewhere: a job to make some quick cash, or pay off student loans, or simply try something new, all too easily turned into a career, to keep up the new mortgage or car payments or habits of one sort or another. Such is the story of adulthood. What was unique, I think, among the cubicles was the absolutely stultifying paralysis which set in beneath all the apparent freedom. There was some sort of compensation at work, as in any fairy tale—Dorian Gray ages in his portrait, not in life; our cubicles were Gray's picture frame, gray indeed, in which each and every one of us gave over some greater or lesser portion of our firmness and elasticity and vigor, and slowly or rapidly petrified, whether we realized it or not.

Those who lost their cubicle jobs quickly enough, or young enough, or who possessed an unusual share of native energy, could start again when they were expelled from the garden—as we all must inevitably be—but this rebirth seldom occurred. Why spend that dream year in Thailand, or go to medical school, or get serious about painting, or take up a stable, gratifying career with the National Park Service, when instead, if you linger around the same bars or network at enough pink-slip parties, another job like the one you lost, but even better paid, is surely awaiting you? But I anticipate; in the early years there were no pink-slip parties, and changing jobs was as easy as buying the next pair of Kenneth Cole shoes, and people believed themselves when they heard themselves say that five more years of this rate of stock appreciation would make them millionaires, or that this economy wouldn't decline like every other economy in the history of the world because it was the *new* economy. In those years, even getting fired—or laid off, or downsized, or restructured, or reorg'd, or realigned, or RIFfed (for "Reduction In Force"), depending on which month your fate was euphemized in—even that was not enough to save you from the syndrome I am describing.

I anticipate in another sense as well: our sluggish dependency set in not when we left our cubicles but earlier, in the Bower of Bliss itself. I saw it everywhere around me, not that I took what I saw to heart, or believed I would be as hamstrung as all that by staying on. There are two kinds of perfect job, I had decided when I started at Prophet: the intrinsically satisfying ones which get you up in the morning on their own account, and the ones which are harmless, which give you enough time and money to lead your real life elsewhere. But is anything truly harmless? Fortunately—unless this too was a self-serving, self-sabotaging delusion—a low voice in my ear always told me that somehow, before it was too late, I would rub my eyes and look around and find myself somewhere new. Yet it was hard not to grow melancholy and restless. I wondered how I could leave a job that was the envy of all my friends, and asked myself why I shouldn't stay, after all I could travel, and write on the side, someday, as a hobby. Was it really so terrible to grow gray among the cubicles, evaporating with my increasing seniority into someone who worked solely at home and allegedly lived there too? A dreary prospect, this, for someone with the youthful idealism I had possessed upon first entering my cubicle and learning that The Internet *Changes* Everything, but which should I trust, youthful idealism or adult comforts?

In the meantime there I was, a tolerably good editor instead of a tolerably poor writer, as old Hawthorne would say. That was all. Outside the Editorial Group's humanistic bubble seethed a salutary world of people who cared little for my or anyone else's literary life, and knew still less. It is always a good, brisk lesson to see how insignificant one's struggles are to those outside one's small circle, and if the men and women of Prophet did not learn that lesson from me, I thoroughly learned it from them. I no longer aspired to see my name blazoned on title pages, meanwhile achieving such fame nevertheless: my name on the credits pages of dozens of books, read by thousands, books explaining how to use a certain database or manage client ROI in a B2B e-business footprint or design a Customer Call Center (CCC). It could now be found as well on hundreds of web pages, bringing a knowledge of my existence, or at least of my name, to millions who had never known of it before, and, I can only assume, will never hear of it again. Once in a great while the aspirations which had earlier seemed so vital revived within me, but my fifteen or twenty hours a week of work never managed to leave me enough time (if that is the right word) to pursue such fancies.

∎

Not the least depersonalizing aspect of life among the cubicles was our subordination to the "latest numbers" mentioned near the start of my tale. Numbers, in their very nature, neither love nor understand us, and it is a strange experience for a person of any dignity to realize that his or her interests are entirely within their control. There were in fact two sets of numbers, from different sources, referred to collectively as The Numbers—sales figures and stock prices and an entire galaxy of other quantities in the real world of business and money and people, and, on the other hand, the goals and projections which as far as I could tell simply sprang full-grown from our Zeus's head: "Next quarter I want a 50% margin in this Line Of Business!" Both sets of numbers were equally sacrosanct, and were treated as stemming from equally infallible authority; there was never the slightest question of, say, deciding that 49.99% was profit enough in this new economic climate and that the publisher I described earlier was a talent worth managing rather than firing. No, failing to meet an arbitrary projection expressed in round numbers would "spook the investor" far more than clear-cutting our internal resources would, and Prophet Corp. prided itself on its frenzies of activity, as vigorous and shortsighted as possible to impress the stockholders and the general public with the mere fact of activity and a few artificial benchmarks of achievement.

The first rounds of RIFs had left the editors untouched, our red ink acting as the mark on the door telling Death to pass this house by. (The metaphor is not quite right: as I have mentioned, our cubicles had no doors.) Editorial Group was simply too mysterious, I think, and too small for its force to be worth reducing. But great was the managerial rejoicing when someone thought of India, timeless homeland of the mysterious and, more importantly, an English-speaking nation with third-world wages. The jarring dissonance of Indian English for readers accustomed to American Business English, which one might perhaps suggest poses problems for the idea of Indian editors; a twelve-and-a-half-hour time difference, making any collaboration or even conversation between writer and editor impossible, except over e-mail; the ability and training of at least some of us on campus—all of these objections were swept aside, if indeed they were ever noticed, and at once our corridor in C wing took on the appearance of a warehouse. Boards nailed across the top and the entrance of each cubicle no longer transformed it into a coffin, but into a packing crate; we were shipped off to India, overnight express, ergonomic chairs and puppy dog calendars and all. The three wise managers who had seen a light in the east and set out to make their offerings there brought numerous gifts, each four feet square and five feet high.

So much for our figurative selves. The real beings—myself and the nun and the wren and the patriarch, no doubt the angels off-campus too—remained safely in place. I cannot speak for anyone else; for myself, I did not remain long. I brushed the sawdust and packing debris from my shoulders and proceeded to stir up some dust from the road onto my shoes. All those names to conjure with in northern California—Adobe, Apple, Hewlett-Packard, NexTel, Oracle, PeopleSoft, Seybold—all those talismanic words: online learning, connectivity, Reusable Content Objects—all those latter-day Ralstons and Hearsts who seemed to play such important roles in the world—how little time it took to detach me from them all, in recollection no less than in deed! My colleagues too are but shadows, barely condensed through my incantations into whatever solidity they may have in this tale and now, like ghosts with their haunting penance fulfilled, released into whatever afterlife it is their fate to occupy. The world of the cubicles lies behind me now like a dream, and to this day I do not know the extent to which I believe in it.

Goldenchain

Anne had planned the trip. Our excuse was my working longer hours than usual but the real reason was that she liked to plan, liked to curl up with coffee and a stack of travel books and imagine all the different possible hotel rooms or sights or cities; I liked to be surprised by what was in front of me. The real real reason was our separation—six weeks later she was leaving New York for good, to stay with her sister and recover from our marriage, and this was to be our last trip together.

The end had come a few months before. I had stopped at a new café on my way home and seen a woman sprawled by herself at a table. A flurry of books and notepads lay in a studied scatter before her, and a cup with its coating of leftover foam; the woman's long, stiff legs reached to the other side under the table while the rest of her body cantilevered back, shoulders pressed into the chair, head held straight up reading documents held in front of her face. Seeing Anne this way, as a stranger—I didn't recognize her at first, there was no reason she should be uptown at this hour, unless for a meeting she hadn't mentioned or I had forgotten—I felt I was seeing her clearly, more clearly than I had in a long time. She was so casual, overly casual, that she seemed defensive, walling her surroundings out instead of relaxing in them, and she inhabited that attitude, that tilt toward the world, with utter familiarity. Her wide straight haircut looked protective, like shoulder pads, with gray rebar reinforcements; she looked older than I remembered, she must have aged with me. When had her face taken on that pinched look, or had it been there all along? No, "pinched" was unfair, but it would soon grow pinched enough at this rate; so far it was just hard. It didn't let you see her fierce, warm intelligence, and it didn't mask it: it hid it in plain sight, like the purloined letter. Her face was fierce, warm intelligence grown hard.

I'm sure she would have been happy to see me, would have relaxed her face into a smile, pulled herself up into her chair and gathered her things to make room for me. But it seemed wrong to intrude on her. It seemed wrong to intrude in a café on my wife of eight years sitting by herself. Here she was, I allowed myself to think, relaxing without me, absorbed in her own life: let her have it. Let her have her time in a new café with documents and notes and a wall around her. I did not want to know this self-contained woman, not nearly as fragile as she always led me to believe, or as I had always imagined. I took my coffee and hurried off. And then I could never tell her I had seen her, because she would ask why I hadn't said hello and I wouldn't be able to answer. Now I had something new to seal up inside myself, to keep from her.

After another grim weekend of useless sniping she called in sick and we walked to our favorite spot in the city, the small lake near 72nd St. in Central Park. Side by side, near each other with the familiarity and intimacy of marriage, hands clenched deep in our own pockets to fight off the cold. Those "Danger — Thin Ice" signs were posted symbolically around the lake, but there were human footprints everywhere on the snowdrifts scattered across the surface, and the people we overheard, while we sat on the bench, all wanted to walk out despite the signs. One bossy eight- or nine-year-old made her dad throw a rock onto the ice, and the father explained as they walked away that "That rock is a lot less heavy than you are, sweetheart." Anne and I walked on, down the winding paths through the mounded stone to the east. Soon we were alone, in what felt like an empty, endless landscape of snow and stone and thin bare branches, but of course in every direction, beyond the trees, rose the skyscrapers of New York.

"Have you thought about what Dr. Anfang said yet?" she asked me.

"I was just going to ask you that."

"Well really it's not up to me."

"Oh, I forgot, it's all about me, like always."

"That's *not* what I meant." Pause. "But it is up to you to decide what you want."

"No, I know. I'm sorry."

"Just . . ." Pause. "What *do* you want?"

For once I could answer I wanted out, and she could hear it as fact, not a threat to repel or a problem to solve. And now, as I said,

I was spending longer hours than usual writing. It had been a cold winter, and not until April had the last snow melted, the cherry trees bloomed, the scarves around people's necks become the kind worn only by women, but by then I was mostly inside. At first I had taken to walking the streets of Manhattan for hours at a time. All the walks had the same rhythm, my rhythm, whether I walked up Riverside Drive past the Church, all the way to the Revolutionary War's Fort Tryon and the robber baron's Cloisters, across from the stark Jersey Palisades far away across the Hudson, or walked east from Columbia into the woods of Morningside Heights, which I had often seen but never entered, and then my reward was the faded dignity of Spanish Harlem before heading down cold Fifth Avenue, or Madison. How different the almost-European streetlife of Amsterdam Avenue from the sleepier brick behemoths of West End. The most immersive was Broadway, of course, a straight shot, past my childhood hangouts from 102nd to 93rd, the smell of 50-cent hot dogs from Gray's Papaya on 72nd, the chaos of Columbus Circle, past the frenzies of midtown to the rambles of lower Manhattan. On one winter walk in widening circles through the brownstone and churchyard neighborhoods around Washington Square I passed the African Museum on 7th St., remembered an editor's recommendation, and stopped in.

.

The museum was practically empty, as it was every time I went back, and the exhibit was Ethiopian healing scrolls: tall narrow strips of thick old parchment, covered in graceful Amharic calligraphy, with islands of images—literally magical drawings and talismans—

embedded in the text, visually bursting out of it. Wise men had made the scrolls for the sick, based on astrological charts, and tailored the scrolls to the same height as the patients themselves, plus a bit more to reach metaphorically over the patient's head around to the back of the neck for extra protection. Few scrolls survive because most people used them until they crumbled; even from a distance, hung high on the museum walls, they worked on me. I could not get enough of them.

The text was soothing too: stretches of black and red, more angular than Arabic, almost talismanic on its own (I don't know Amharic). The pictures were representational and abstract at once—mostly angels, but more like Klee's than Hallmark's: angels pared down to their emotional core, beneficent yet childlike. Or maybe they make you feel childlike. Their heads are too large for their bodies and their eyes are too large for their heads; they loom, like a buried first memory of a parent. Sometimes there is only a face—two eyes and a double vertical line for a nose; sometimes there are only eyes, and the paintings become impossible to interpret. A face at the center of an eight-pointed star, where each point loops into an eye: is it a cherub with eight wings, or Solomon's seal, or a devil caught in Solomon's net and guarded by the eyes of angels, or God and the bearers of his throne, or the demon Werzelys and his soldiers, or the "face of man," the face of the talisman? Nobody knows in much detail what the different symbols and patterns mean, but it doesn't much matter: the pictures are magical: they don't *mean,* they *are,* they *work.*

The faces of the saints and angels on the scrolls are round, yet slender and delicate, like those of the Ethiopians I know except deep red. When I saw them I remembered the first time I saw a solid red wall, in a friend's apartment with a few black and white photographs hung near the center. How calming it was. When did red become the color of the devil and stop signs and fire engines? Here the devil cavorts in a flat, depth-destroying black.

It is strange to see devils look out at you from healing scrolls, and this too no one can quite explain. In one image, the devil is pale cool gray and crammed in a box, arms and legs doubled back, with yellow chains across his shins and thighs and teeth. His box is itself a chain of eyes, with four cooperating angels holding in outstretched arms four diagonal crosses which seal the corners of Satan's cage. The angels are flat on the picture plane, as in most of these images, but here they are shown only from the arms and shoulders up, as if they were flying straight towards us with the rest of their bodies stretched out behind them. Their armspans form the arcs of a circle, so that the image as a whole is a cross (the angels' wings), and in the cross a diagonal square of crosses and a pale blue circle, and in the circle a square of eyes, and in the center the devil: asymmetrical, in profile, but safely chained.

I returned to the museum again and again to look at the scrolls; I got books from the library and made color copies. Throughout the scrolls, I saw a comforting drive for completeness, for covering every base. The gray devil is enclosed in layer after layer; in another talisman, a demon is trapped by seven uprights and seven rungs, all obstacles in the enemy's way, and if he overcomes one he will probably be stopped by the next. If he has some protective power against the talisman, it probably uses a single color, but the talisman has several colors just in case. The diagonals connecting the uprights and rungs are supports for the talisman's owner, as well as crossed wings which cover the demon's flight, as well as scissors to cut up sickness. The inscriptions, too, try to name and control everything: "By the one God, by the Trinity, and by the five nails of the cross, let demons, evil eyes, headaches, pain in the side and in the stomach, rheumatism of the hands and of the feet, fevers and malaria, sorcerers and sorceresses, *dasek* and *gudale,* Dedeq and the demon of noon, *zar* and demons and the spell-casters, not approach the soul and the body of your servant!"

But the overarching philosophy seems to be one of containment. Even the use of double lines, I later read, is so the lines can contain while they separate: instead of a stark division between two regions on the parchment, the lines are regions of their own, colored in, harmonizing with other elements in the talisman. Angels carry seals, rarely swords; evil is not to be battled or destroyed, but banished or boxed in. The scrolls are not designed to strengthen the self of the sick petitioner with infusions of holiness, as in other Christian traditions I knew about; they don't trust our own ability to fight, they are more modest, simply trying to keep damage under control, ward it off.

The piece I was writing about the scrolls was on spec—the latest of my poor business decisions as a writer—but at least that meant there was no deadline, and my reading and writing could expand to fill as much space as I offered them. I looked out my window, at the top of the opposite building and the bottom of the sky. I looked at the photocopies taped to the wall, or shut my eyes and listened to the spring rain type its sentences onto the window and wash them away unread. I sat in the study and read and looked at the photocopies taped to the wall; I had fetched all the books from the library already so there was no need to go for a walk, and besides it was raining. I didn't know what to shape the piece into—a review, an essay, maybe even the novel I still wanted (and want) to write, or at least a short story. Something about the subject gave me no choice but to see where it would take me.

■

I used to talk over all my writing projects with Anne, but this one I kept to myself, except when my mother passed through town. She was moving again. Every four or five years except during her childhood and mine, each of which had kept her in place for almost twenty, just when she was settling into what could be called a community there was some reason to uproot herself and move on: politics, climate, an opportunity somewhere else, always somewhere else. She had lived on five continents, in three quarters of the world, and often mentioned Chile or Brazil which would complete the set. Her self-reinvention seemed courageous, almost heroic, to most of my friends; she kept few of her own. She was born and raised in South Africa, left the week she graduated high school, couldn't wait to leave, and I admired how successfully she had cut me off from the psychoses of South African culture in only one generation. But I sometimes felt that was not all she cut me off from: I stayed in one New York apartment throughout my childhood but never really put down roots, which was one reason I decided to keep the lease when she moved to Yellow Springs, Ohio, three moves ago. Now, after eight or nine years in Europe—four or five in Madrid, four or five in London—the English weather had proven too much for someone from Africa and she was moving to California, into a beautiful, isolated house on the side of a mountain near Santa Cruz.

She was in New York just long enough for a cab from the airport and lunch at Obaa Koryoe in the border zone between the Upper West Side and Harlem, and I told her about the healing scrolls. Those aren't the only two options, she said, much more engaged than when I had told her about Anne and me a few minutes earlier. There's another possibility besides battle or containment, fight or flight, you know. What about the homeopathic approach? Instead of trying to shut out the sickness, you let a little of it in, acknowledge the devil within you instead of repressing it, and that's what makes you stronger.

I never know what to make of these moments from my mother. I take the mind seriously as my lens or grid for viewing the world; in someone like Anne it is just as important but more playful somehow. For me, a businessman deciding what tier of power tie to wear for today's meeting; for Anne, a duchess dressing up for the ball. My mother is more like those young men who rail against people judging others by their appearance—they themselves pay attention to what's *important,* and dress in whatever ugly clothes are around. But in rare moments their thrown-on hand-me-downs come together into a look, a neodisjunctivist style all their own, and those are the moments like my mother's insights.

That night I dreamt I was making a scroll for her. I was both the sage with the paintbrush and myself outside the scene watching everyone—this has always been the structure of my dreams. I watched my paintbrush glide across the paper, never dipped in the inks, but the scroll still appeared in both black and red with multi-colored pictures and talismans. The wise man draped her head with it but my mother must have grown, or else he had made an unprecedented mistake: the scroll was a foot too short, it could reach over her head or protect her feet but not both. I was furious at his incompetence, livid. But my mother tugged the scroll down so it covered her from neck to feet, so she could see, then set off down the dirt path home.

Aside from the pun between *path home* and *homeopathic,* and the obvious wish for my writing to be effortless, I think most of the dream came from another part of our talk. As I told her more about the scrolls, she was most excited about a detail I mentioned in passing: patients carried the scrolls with them, rolled up in red leather tubes at the ends of a long loop of string, like European hunting horns. It's like a box that keeps others out but doesn't box you in, my mother said. That's the problem with walls you build, they trap you as much as anybody else. This portable protection reminded her of diving bells, or those underwater cages on nature shows with a photographer inside, lowered into the water and pulled around while the sharks attack in vain, breaking their teeth on the thick metal bars as they lunge and gnash. And the photographer travels wherever he wants, or wherever he's towed.

■

Anne and I had never seen the Pacific Northwest, so we—or she—decided on San Juan Island in Puget Sound; there would be whale-watching for her, wildflowering for me, we could bike around the island and take walks along the coasts, and go sea-kayaking, and have done at least one more of the things we always thought we'd do together. We drove our rented Toyota north from Seattle through a landscape like upstate New York, but starker somehow, more American Sublime. Rapeseed lined the roads: sprawling woody shrubs dotted with hard yellow pompomlets. And the smell was different too—the hint of ocean, not pine; not dirt and leaves, but bark and earth.

Stopping at a mall to use the bathrooms, we ended up in a clothing store, Anne for the last time picking out shirts for me to buy. (We had already started thinking of things as "the last time . . .")

"This one's nice!"

"That green one?"

"It'll match your eyes, try it on."

"But you know I hate sideways stripes, they look stupid if they're thin and too preppy if they're wide."

"Just try it, ok? It'll look so nice."

This kind of shopping was a holdover from the early days of our relationship, like so much else. But I did like the shirts, and in fact I am wearing one now as I write.

We drove onto the ferry, looked at the islands sliding slowly by in the sound and ate overpriced hot dogs on the mezzanine deck. We eavesdropped and made up stories about the other passengers: the commuters, the three fabulous retirees arguing madly over the cribbage board, those tourists (we didn't count as "tourists," of course). After a short drive south on San Juan Island, but longer than we expected from the maps she had shown me on the plane, we were on a long dirt driveway. Quail with Dr. Seuss topknots zigzagged crazily back and forth in front of the car. A three-story Victorian stood alone at the end of a field which sloped downward into the fog and gave an uncanny impression of space: it was not like someone's backyard, literally or conceptually fenced in; not like whatever smallish portions of wilderness adjoin the other houses I've seen—this house was on the edge of a world. There was a garden plot in front, but I have never seen a garden so contained, so clearly a pocket of cultivation barely noticed by an ocean of meadow. Next to the garden was a beautiful tree I didn't recognize—squat like a cherry tree, but with thicker, grayer branches and trunk, like an oak; droopy like lilac but with long yellow strings of flowers instead of clusters hanging down from the crown. The tree stood out too, modestly primordial.

We met the owners, Mr. and Mrs. Inoue, carried the bags up to our second-floor room, and began our vacation. Everything until then had been part of our lives, contiguous with it, but the rest of the trip seemed, to us both, a world apart. The unknown future sloped gently away like the Inoues' meadow. Without a connection to our future this long weekend unmoored itself from our past as well: it felt different. Or it felt the same, but differently, more intensely the same. We did everything together—Anne used to say that I was always pulling away, retreating into myself, disengaging from her and from our marriage, but that time was past. That night and the next, Anne and I watched the roof grow darker green and browner and the porch lights grow brighter on a cottage on the other side of the field, to the south; we saw a lighthouse across the bluing sound, and Brewer's blackbirds in the yellow-fringed tree, otherwise nothing. Time will go slower, Anne told me, if we just don't do anything.

Even so, beneath the whole trip lay its lastness, like an undertow, connecting our time there to an antithesis of future. And our past was a part of us too. I found myself constantly angry with my mother, for example, and had several imagined conversations with her, in which I spent more time replaying my reprimands than imagining her replies—always a bad sign. Why did she have to keep trying someplace else? Why couldn't she give anywhere a chance? ("Why should I?") Don't you miss settling in to a place, working your way down to the bedrock? Aren't you lonely? ("Not really . . .") I wanted to chain her up in a little box, angels with crosses sealing the corners. I would have been so unhappy in her life, and because so much inside me pulls me in that direction I had to resist, not acknowledge how she could be different, how she could be happy with what would have made me so terribly sad.

When my sister Kim decided to marry her high school boyfriend I think she was doing the same thing. I wasn't home much then—home, along with my mother and sister, had moved out from under me, away from New York to Ohio—but I do remember a holiday dinner, Thanksgiving or Christmas, with the five of us. After Lars left (he, like Kim, still living at home) and Anne went up to bed, the family talked for a while and my mother tried to dissuade Kim from taking this step so soon.

"When won't it be too soon, Mom? What are *you* still waiting for?"

Kim couldn't wait to leave, put the chaos behind her and settle down. In reacting against, of course, she was only repeating our mother, fleeing as she had. It made me wonder about all those old sayings like "blood is thicker than water." Kim and I fell out of touch, absorbed in the worlds we were trying to make for ourselves. Then she left Lars and moved off to the city, after what I think was an abortion, my mother was vague and I heard about it only through her. I had been meaning to write Kim for months now, maybe years already, but hadn't. My stationery even came along to Puget Sound. I unpacked it and there it lay in its box the whole trip.

When Anne and I woke up in our room for the last time, she called me to the window, startled, and we could see miles and miles of the Olympic Mountains, sheer snowcapped rock glinting blue and white in the sunlight, behind a thin, foreshortened strip of water past the end of the meadow. Over breakfast we marveled to the Inoues at the view, and they told us a dust storm in China two months before had crossed the Pacific and made it impossible to see the view until today. This reminded Mr. Inoue of their own story: they had lived seventeen years together in San Francisco, had known for a fact that they would live there forever, until they visited San Juan Island for a long weekend, looked at each other on the plane ride back, and put their house in San Francisco up for sale that same week. When they bought this place they had seen it only in the fog, had been promised "a view of the water" but expected a sliver from tiptoes, you know how real estate agents are. They bought it anyway—the house and its meadow with the yellow-fringed tree were enough. The fog cleared a few days after they moved in, and they looked out at the breathtaking panorama.

"It's called laburnum," Mrs. Inoue replied to my next question, about the tree, "or goldenrain, or goldenchain. This one is defective; the chains can grow up to two or three feet long. Go look at the ones near the center of the island."

That afternoon Anne wanted to go down to the water to watch for whales, perhaps her greatest consolation for the world of people she found herself in. Her sister had phoned at the end of breakfast, they talked for a long time as always, and when she came up to the room where I lay on the bed looking out at the mountains I could tell she had been crying, then trying to hide it.

"You OK?"

"What do you mean?"

"You look upset."

"No . . ."

It was going to be one of those fights, where she wouldn't even admit we were fighting or that anything was wrong. I was too tired of it to play both sides myself, so I pretended not to notice, which made her mad at my lack of perceptiveness, even though she was the one hiding things in the first place. I would pay for it later. It was all so familiar.

"How's your sister?" I asked, brightly.

And when Anne went whale-watching I went to climb Mt. Taylor, hardly a Mt. but one of the biggest hills on the island, near the center. On the way up I stopped at the British Camp Cemetery; from a plaque at another park I had already learned that Puget Sound was contested territory until 1872, when Kaiser Wilhelm adjudicated between Canada (Great Britain) and the U.S. The only casualty in the conflict was a British Hudson Bay Company pig, shot and killed by an American settler in 1859, hence "The Pig War." Yet people die too, it seems, even young British soldiers, "Age 28, from Derby, England," so far from home, in a place so unimaginable to their families. Now they overgrow their own gravestones in a strange grassy grove on the hillside, enclosed in a white picket fence and a humming scent the transmuted young men release into the air themselves.

I never found any goldenchains, but I did find a new kind of view after the short hike to the top. It was partly a trick of scale: the rest of San Juan and the dozens of other islands looked like continents, so the sound looked like an ocean and my view seemed to reach farther than ever before. But surrounding this sea with its feel of infinity were mountains on all sides—Olympics to the south, Cascades to the east, Canada's Gulf Islands to the west and mainland to the north—so you felt infinity and containment at once. Not a view from a mountaintop, with the land spread out before you, not a view of the ocean lapping out into the curved distance, but both, like being at the center of those circular medieval maps, bounded but somehow more boundless than our globes or square Mercators. Like abandoning everything to move to a house in the fog on a faraway island, together.

I passed the cemetery again on my way down but I didn't stop. I went back to the hotel and phoned my mother to wish her well. I'll come out and see your new place next month, I said, once you've had some time to settle in. I promise. The streaks of white on the Olympics turned slowly purple in the late afternoon sun.

A Guide to San Francisco

This morning I took the bus to work in the outer Richmond, down the long wide avenues out toward the sea, and now I am waiting in a bar for my friend. It's a bar in the Mission with a fat, happy pig instead of a shingle hanging down from the night. My friend arrives and I start to tell him about the gray sky, telephone wires, and other important matters.

1   THE SKY

Like stones at the seaside, a December sky like this afternoon's gets its beauty from wetness. Dull sandstone buildings regain their sandy glory, the glory of a sunlit beach, while the sky is the color the sea must be, still and gray under an afternoon sky. The buildings and the sky are in strange resonance, and between the two the leaves on the trees drip with green: the air is too saturated to hold more color. It was late in the afternoon, late in the year, the rains that have lasted all week and threatened all day were late to arrive, everything was late today and at last it got through to me, I wondered what I was late for. Either the sky has been this color before—so gray it's blue against the rich yellow sandstone—and I have not noticed, or I have done something wrong with my life and never been granted this color until now. The wind picked up as I hurried down the street, shoulders hunched over, fists in my pockets.

2   THE CABLES

On the bus to or from work, my eyes are drawn to the geography above the city: cables, phone wires, streetcar lines, rows of poles like freeways and nodes like traffic jams where thirty or forty or even fifty lines snarl into a single tangle. I want a map—in a different color, maybe an overlay or transparency on the street map. Guana-juato, a city roughly halfway from Guadalajara to Mexico City in a long ravine, spilling its color up either side, has maps like that. A network of tunnels runs under the whole city, mostly for cars but also for people; as you walk around town you come across passageways into the cliffs or stairwells like those leading down into subway stations. The maps of Guanajuato you get from the tourist office are printed in green and white, green for below-ground like a prophecy of spring.

This makes me imagine a man who spends his days in the other parallel city a dozen feet below, not above, the streets of San Francisco. In the subway tunnels, among the gas mains, phone cables (again), foundations, and their natural counterparts: water tables, strata, roots. In a room you can reach only through his office in the Department of Public Works stands his private work, a three-dimensional model of the underground—a grid of clear plastic rods, a half-cube fifteen or twenty feet square and about eight feet high, with colored wires that represent all the different burrowings. The model is not to scale, just as relief maps have to exaggerate a thousandfold—a globe to scale would feel smooth as marble, Everest and the Marianis Trench and all. The horizontal overpowers the vertical in this as in all things. The colored filaments snaking through the clear grid would have to be microscopically thin for a scale model of even the downtown district to fit in his office, but aside from that the model is perfect, as perfect as he can make it.

It is almost impossible for anyone except him and me to recognize in these fragile, widely spaced lines the thick, earthy claustrophobia of artificially lit tunnels that one may have seen, or traveled through, or built. But he translates in the opposite direction: whenever he is below-ground, he not only thinks but sees and, as it were, dreams in the language of his map.

I feel that this is the only sense of art: to create an inner universe we prefer to the other one. If I could write enough and make it true enough then perhaps I could have what I write before my eyes always. After looking at enough van Goghs you go out into the world and everything seems like a van Gogh, and what else is Paradise?

3 PENTIMENTO

The first time I visited San Francisco, as a high school student, I took the ferry over glittering waters to the western edge of the city, walked around downtown and then back toward Coit Tower to the south, which I climbed at the end of the day in a cold summer wind. I still remember the bright colors of the ferry building, the cable-car terminus at the bottom of the hill, metal rails in the brick streets, white flags flapping, the grassy field to one side. Except the ferry arrives at the east shore of San Francisco, Coit Tower rises up to the north, and I have never again found the green field at the base of the hill, the streetside benches I sat on, the record store I stopped into. I also remember climbing a steep San Francisco hill and reaching a pier, so I know how trustworthy these memories must be. The sea is found at sea level, I'm afraid this fact of everyday experience outweighs memory, but I need only recall my first San Francisco and it overpowers my experience, even when I am on the real streets, at the real Coit Tower, or the ferry building.

4 MILLEFLEUR

Westward the course of the 31 bus takes its way, parallel to Golden Gate Park a few blocks to the south. The streets are wide in the Richmond and all but empty, which makes this neighborhood feel like The West: tumbleweeds and a stagecoach, a warm wind blowing through town with an eerie whistle. Endless two- or three-storey wooden houses, chipper pinks or yellows often faded to gray or white, follow after each other with that purely American disregard of space: there is no pressure to build high or close, no hurry to get to the grocery store or acupuncture center at the end of the block. The architects or city planners, in a purely American stupor, just kept on going. What businesses there are out here are in residential buildings, too, in the area's attempt to make this depressing street livable.

Still, I prefer the 31 bus on Balboa to the 5 along the park, because this way, if I sit on the left, a gap between the buildings opens up every block and a forest fills it, wild with mystery.

One day in the 1950s, a student of Nabokov's came into his office and asked for advice on becoming a writer. *Lolita* had not yet let this distant, bossy Russian professor retire to the Montreux he deserved. Nabokov swiveled in his wooden desk chair, or so I imagine it, and pointed to the tree outside the window (what kind of tree it was has not come down to posterity). The professor's imperious question: "Can you tell me what kind of tree that is?" The student looks politely, for appearance's sake, before answering no. "Then you'll never be a writer."

I don't know the kinds of tree in Golden Gate Park, for me they are simply lush and dark at the bottom and plunge up at the top toward the heights of San Francisco, but I have to admit I have never been as moved by the realists or the world-creating fabulists as I am by the pattern-makers. Burgundian tapestry or complicated wallpaper fills the space that's there with treeness, and in the gaps between the buildings on Balboa lie textures of green that set me dreaming.

I never walk down Balboa or Cabrillo all the way to the ocean, to the surf shop with its surf-shop smell, but it is important to know you can.

"Sounds like a good day," my friend says, a literary type. Like San Francisco he has two personas: rugged-outdoorsy and stylish-nerdy. Tonight he is wearing his black plastic glasses and a button-down, short-sleeve shirt, foregoing Sierra Nevadas to drink intellectual Belgian beers whose names he pronounces correctly.

The glass doors in front are open; the first third of indoors might as well be outdoors. Our table sits right on the fault line. Behind my friend is the long, low bar with no barstools, where you order but do not stand. There are enough café-style tables for everyone, especially on a warm night like tonight.

I try again to describe the despair of the December sky, the disorientation around Coit Tower and my nonexistent dream-coast at the top of a hill.

"That reminds me of Guanajuato," he says.

"I've never been."

"An old silver town, very rich under the Spanish, so there's incredible colonial architecture there now: basilicas, courtyards, tiles, high ceilings. (But low mirrors—I had to bend down to see my face in every mirror in Mexico.) Diego Rivera was born in Guanajuato, and there's a small museum in the house where he was born. The day I visited turned out to be his birthday! The other reigning spirit is Don Quijote—he lives in the Quijote Iconography Museum where every painting, drawing, sculpture, plate, porcelain egg, and macramé wall hanging shows Quijote or Sancho Panza or Dulcinea, or windmills, or the burning of the books. A strange pair, Rivera and Quijote. The muralist makes worlds and the sad knight gets lost in them."

Behind my back is Mexican San Francisco: stray dogs; middle-aged couples taking their *passeo*; a mariachi trio wandering with their instruments between the Mexican restaurants and the white bars. My friend tells me to look—across the street a revival meeting has started up, in Spanish, complete with singing and a full band. I get up to use the bathroom but it's out of order, instead I have to follow a long narrow corridor off to the side, behind and parallel to the bar. It ends in a turn and a door, open onto the night at this end too. Outside, the ambient light of the city is dim but the way is too narrow to get lost in: down a short flight of wobbly wooden stairs, along a tiny fenced walkway snaking through the dead space behind all the buildings on the block, and finally up a short flight of rickety stairs to a shed with a thin sickle moon carved out of the door and nothing inside but a toilet and a metal hook on the door and an eye on the doorframe. I pull a long chain to flush from a tank above my head.

When I get back to the table, my friend starts to tell me about the book he is working on, set in Silicon Valley and the biotech complexes unsafely springing up on the landfill downtown where public housing was supposed to go. His descriptions remind me of everything I hate about living here: too expensive, too divisive, too new.

"I need to get out of this city," I say.

"How can you want to leave San Francisco? People come to San Francisco, they don't leave."

I barely pay attention to this conversation, the same one I have with all of my friends these days. I am looking over my friend's shoulder; from where I sit I can see people reach the locked bathroom door, turn down the hall, and come back several minutes later with a bright expression on their faces, breath quick, eyes adjusted to the dim outdoor light. They have had an unexpected adventure, groping their way in the dark, climbing up and down stairs in the night.

Dialogue Between the
Two Chief World Systems

I first heard L's story— . . . but let me begin at the beginning.

It was near the end of one of those months when I had, as I liked to put it, "forgotten how to read" after a period of creative work which left me drained. I spent afternoons sitting at the dining table, each day the vase of flowers spread wider than the day before; in the Asian rug on the dining room floor two googly-eyed dragons with clawed feet chased each other playfully around the yellow background, through woven clouds, like a parable of time. At night, when the solitude got to be too much to bear, I explored the nether reaches of my local bar's beer list, in uncanny concoctions compiled by the establishment's most sadistic bartender, Kate, with all the nefarious ingenuity of her unbridled scientific curiosity.

When my colleague J walked in one night it was the first time in half a year that I had seen him, but this in itself was not unusual.

He was often possessed by strange fixations and disappeared into his eclectic apartment for months at a time to cheerfully pursue an arcane dissertation on "The Frame Narrative and the Nature of the Literary Object" or other projects. No, what was unusual that night was a glint in his eye that darkly suggested a certain desperation I had never seen in him.

He joined me, I warned him with a shudder away from Kate's framboise geueze flambée, and tried to find out what was wrong. His habitual reserve crumbled under the pressure of his dark secret; he needed to talk, yet the remarkable nature of his tale made it hard for him to get the words out at all. At last he related what follows, which I will put into first-person form for convenience, omitting his many hesitations, stammers, and lapses into gloomy silence:

"I was sitting at this very bar when she came over to talk, the demon! She recognized me from a lecture earlier that day and wanted to introduce herself. Her name, she said, was Zsófi Szechenyi, deeply implausible as only a Hungarian name can be, and her face was even more melodic, with pert cheeks and mobile lips, like a daguerreotype come to life in the dark oval frame of her hair . . . But what does it matter how she looked?" (J interrupted himself), "this isn't that kind of story.

"She said she was in grad school too, specializing in Adriatic literature and stuck here for the year, to the great dismay of her Balkan husband back in— . . . Enough of that! What matters is, we drank and talked about our work and our intellectual passions—both of us thrilled to find another of the rare few grad students left who have any—and, a crowd of empty beer bottles and peach margarita glasses clanking on the table between our elbows later, she asked me if I knew 'Dialogue Between the Two Chief World Systems,' her favorite story.

" 'Great title!' I said."

("It *is* a great title," I said to J.)

" 'It's Galileo's,' she said with a smile that made me forget who Galileo was. 'His treatise on Copernican and Ptolemaic astronomy.'

" 'That makes it even better,' I said, but she already knew it.

" 'The author is an Italian writer, L. In fact, I don't know if the story has been translated into English, but it's certainly in Hungarian and probably French and German as well.' And she told me about it, with her mobile lips and dancing eyes . . .

" 'It's about a sailor on a long ocean voyage. There's this friend of his, a sort of father figure—I don't remember all the details exactly' (she said" (J said) ") 'but they're stuck in close quarters for a year or two and to pass the time the friend teaches him some obscure language he's picked up in the course of his travels, Tibetan, or maybe it's Persian. The main character learns the language, with its unimagined expressive possibilities, and begins to write poetry in Persian or whatever: beautiful, heartbreaking poetry. The friend jumps ship or dies or something and during the rest of the voyage the main character crafts an epic, unsurpassed in its grandeur and power since Homer, at least that's how it seems to him. Eventually, on land again, he tries to publish his poem and realizes that it isn't in Persian; he consults linguists, translators, and experts of all sorts, only to discover that his epic poem is not in any language whatsoever. The sailor friend had made it up, or unintentionally scrambled different languages together so thoroughly that the strands could no longer be disentangled, they were blended together into a pure elixir. The main character is left with his poems in a language that even he is starting to forget, since he cannot read it or speak it for reinforcement. Finally he visits an eminent critic to have him judge whether the poems are genuine art—a passage of the poetry is actually quoted in the story, in the nonexistent language—and the critic is forced to admit that the poems may in fact be art despite being written in an untranslatable private language. This satisfies the writer but drives him slightly mad . . .'

"Even after the rest of our night together, with its several hitherto unsampled pleasures, the fantastic story she told me is what captured my imagination. When I left the hotel room the next afternoon I returned home and wrote for days, I stayed in my apartment and worked for weeks, she had told the story in such depth and it was so vivid in my mind.

"But the story! That unspeakably diabolical . . . !!"

He calmed down and began again. "After the intellectual adventure of those two weeks in my apartment I went to the library to look up L's story. It didn't exist. I read L's complete works in Italian, tracked down every extant translation of his fiction into any language, then broadened my search. I looked up Galileo's title—actually in English it's 'Dialogue Concerning the Two Chief World Systems,' not 'Dialogue Between': an important difference, with its outside, framing perspective, but never mind—and I sought out and read any short story with a remotely similar title. Finally, I talked to experts in the national literatures of every Adriatic country from Italy to Greece; even Slovenia's paltry twenty-nine miles of coastline was enough to prompt a two-week e-mail exchange with the National and University Library in Ljubljana. It turned up nothing. Zsófi, or whatever her name really is, had meanwhile, according to the people in her department, returned to Montenegro; I have not been able to track her down despite my furious efforts."

I could restrain myself no longer and interrupted my friend. "But what's the matter?" I asked. "You can write this brilliant story yourself, you practically have tonight."

"What's the matter?!" he shouted, with a despairing glance up and down the now almost empty bar. "After I heard L's story—oh, if only it was!—after I heard it I could write at last, everything fell into place.

"I had already written several chapters of my dissertation on frame narratives: one about Hawthorne's memoir 'The Custom-House,' which frames *The Scarlet Letter*; one on a slow, circling story about mothers and mountains by Yasushi Inoue; one on Nabokov's dizzying little 'A Guide to Berlin'—have I told you this already? How far along was I the last time we spoke?"

"You had finished those and were working on a chapter about a novella whose main character is writing a book with the same title as the novella."

"Yes, 'Gide's *Marshlands* and the Paludic Object,'" he said, disappointingly unimpressed by my powers of recall. "Gide never makes it clear what the *Marshlands* book which the character is writing is like, or what his own book *Marshlands* is about for that matter. All the narrator says is that 'watching the insects—the emotion I have in the presence of delicate gray things—is what gave me the idea of writing *Marshlands*.' So the literary object as such is indistinct, low-lying, in a narrow tonal range: pale blues and greens and browns. Writing isn't spectacle, it's a delicate gray thing; it doesn't stand out against a background, it is its ambience. But this was all intuition and editorializing, not an argument: the central chapter of my dissertation, the central connections, were missing. With L's story I could prove it."

J launched into a complicated syllogism which I half followed and half pretended to follow, to the effect that L's story reduced to absurdity the idea that a piece of writing has its source in the writer. ". . . And that's the chapter I'd been trying to write for years. It was genius, at least it came out as close to genius as I can get—it says everything I have to say. But if the story doesn't exist, then my work will mean nothing. My work *means* nothing."

"Still, why not write the story yourself? That way your chapter has something to analyze."

Almost as soon as the words left my mouth I realized how ludicrous the suggestion was; J looked at me with a wry smile. The evidentiary weight of such a story would be less than minimal, while a chapter analyzing his own fiction would make J a laughingstock in his department and beyond. I was stunned as the scope of my friend's troubles began to dawn on me.

We sat in a silence broken only by the raising and lowering of our glasses and sporadic expostulations of outrage and disbelief from J.

"There is," I said at last, "only one solution. Every other possibility is excluded, and when logic dictates, we must submit. One: Your great chapter must be preserved. Two: It requires the existence of this story, 'Dialogue Between the Two Chief World Systems.' Said story has not yet been written, except perhaps by the seductive Zsófi Szechenyi, who has vanished without a trace. You cannot write it yourself, for practical and no doubt psychological reasons of your own, although you seem perfectly able to live it. Therefore: Three: Someone else needs to write the story. You can wait until it's published before you submit your dissertation, and that'll give you a chapter on contemporary fiction too, which can only help your chances on the job market. Now either you can wait and hope some Borges character comes along to re-create the story or you can take matters into your own hands."

Ah, the days of our youth, hurtling by and now gone forever! Such clarity, such vigor! A bar tab with Kate meant nothing, the life of the mind was our everything.

The next morning found us in the office of the head of the Creative Writing Program at our university. The art of literature withheld no secrets from this man; the literary current of our great nation surged with assurance through him into the well-crafted poems and short stories of his students.

The great writer was no longer young, but not yet old, with blond, graying hair swept back from his forehead; a wide, square face; a permanent, teethy smile—he seemed to be going for a leonine effect, but to me it came off merely feline, and I always half expected him to start licking the back of his hand and scrubbing his face with it. He kept eye contact with you through his invisible-rim glasses much longer than most people did, so that it seemed a conscious policy of his, and he either had or affected a chronic, delicate cough.

"It's a fine story, definitely publishable, ckuhhh," he said and coughed. "Love the title."

"But it hasn't been written!" I described J's dilemma.

"A unique, ckuhh, challenge," he admitted, sympathetic uncertainty tinging the expression on his face. "But what do you want me to do?"

"Assign your students to write it. As you say yourself, when the story is worked out properly it will definitely be publishable, so the students have as much to gain as J does."

"But that would be plagiarism," the great writer said.

"I can unequivocally guarantee that this story has never been published," J said loudly, and summarized his research.

"A story needn't have been, ckuhh, published for it to be plagiarized, anymore than a term paper which a student pays someone to write from scratch. What makes something plagiarism is that the story is not one's own."

"What's the difference? It's like when," I spoke from experience, "when you wake up from a dream with a beautiful idea but you don't want to write it down because it doesn't feel yours. And that's true, it didn't come from 'you,' but you have as much of a right to write it as anyone. Consider this Zsófi Szechenyi as a muse, a figment—" J glared at me— "and then J in turn is another muse for your students. You're not against inspiration from the muse, are you?"

The great writer paused for a few moments and blinked several times behind his glasses, smile stuccoed to his face. "Here in the Creative Writing Program," he began, as though everything we had said were nothing, "we not only encourage every one of our students to find his or her own voice, we teach them how. Ckuhhh. Everyone has a unique, personal gift inside them, a story that is theirs alone to tell: my highly trained faculty and I teach our students the process, but we cannot give them the content. Much less foist off someone else's imaginary story on them."

"I beg to differ," said J. "There is no literary creation from inside you: every word in the language, after all, comes from other people. Creativity is description and organization, not invention—taking what comes in and framing it."

"A writer takes in only what is inside him already. Or her. Anything else in the world they won't see or hear. We follow our own tracks through life, our observations make a chain, and the phenomenon or fact that cannot be linked with the rest we simply do not notice."

"That describes the reader, not the writer. What your point shows is precisely that even if a writer could invent something new, no reader would understand it," I said, delighted with my sophistry.

"Mere sophistry," the great writer said, as if reading my mind. "No one is pretending that our stories come from an alien galaxy, with no link at all to the social world. The fact remains that every writer's recombination of reality, if you want to call it that, their mode of organizing and, yes, framing the world is their own, as individual as their fingerprints or DNA."

"So what can you teach?" I was flustered by his cool demolition of my house of cards.

"We help every classroom team member find, ckuhh, their own voice with a proven course of study that involves" (he had given this speech before) "free-writing quotas, twice-weekly workshops, assigned reading, and extensive one-on-one meetings with our experienced faculty. You know that."

"*Free* writing," I scoffed.

"Let me make sure I understand you correctly," J spoke up. "You assign reading because once your students read something they internalize it, take it in and naturalize it, so to speak. Whatever calls to them was them already, or at least it's them now; anything outside them is by definition irrelevant to their work."

"Something like that," the great writer said, dabbing his forehead with a handkerchief. "I wouldn't put it, ckuhhh, in exactly those terms . . ."

"My question is whether you have your students read to find out something about the outside world or something about themselves."

"Both," the great writer said.

"How can you tell?" I pounced. "They read a writer and start trying to write like the newly revealed part of themselves which is similar to that writer, but which was allegedly there all along? Wouldn't it make more sense to say that the writer's work changed them?"

J waved my argument aside. "That's an old paradox about teaching and learning. It goes back to Plato, where Socrates argues that Meno's slave cannot really be learning geometry, he must be remembering what he knew already in the lost world of Forms. It's the same paradox with writing, and painting, and piano lessons, and any other kind of teaching. You're going to lose this one," J said to me, "because people do change and improve and learn, it's pointless to try to deny that it's possible."

The writer and I both nodded in agreement, I reluctantly, he with fierce vindication.

"My point, though," J went on, "is that writing is different. Here, let me show you." He ruffled through his messenger bag, found the page that he wanted, yanked it out of the chapter, and slid it across the great writer's desk:

written language is cut off from the speaker, so it may seem impersonal but it carries its originator's world in every world, as Bakhtin shows.[67] Thus it is personal and impersonal at once, or in a sense orphaned— with parents, but parents it does not know. That is Plato's metaphor: anything written down "rolls around indiscriminately," "it doesn't know to whom it should speak and to whom it should not"; when "attacked unfairly," writing "always needs its father's support" (*Phaedrus* 275e).

This support is what the frame narrative supplies; any piece of writing is framed by the author, in several senses. (1) Like the "framers" of the Constitution, the writer constitutes his or her writing: at the inaugural moment of modern English poetry, for instance, "Well [could] he tune his pipe, and frame his stile" (Spenser, *Shepheardes Calender*, Januarye, l. 10). One meaning of "frame" in the *OED* is to speak—"To form, articulate, utter (words, sounds): **1609** 'God answered by a voice framed by an Angel' "—to speak, that is, in the sense of expressing words as "articulated" or jointed, words in a structure, a worldview. Language is always framed; it depends on the author / progenitor's structuring, his putting it together. Thus (2) the writer's intention, the paternal authorization of the text's world, puts a frame around the piece of writing, and Borges's "Pierre Menard" lays out quite clearly that to change the authorial frame changes the writing itself. In the history of the word, this meaning of "frame" came later: "to frame" originally meant to prepare, and what needed preparation the most in that culture was, it seems, the wood for a house—timber was "framed" or made ready, and then reared or set up. The noun usages "structure" or "armature," and eventually a picture frame, come from that. Finally, (3) the writer makes the text take the rap, "frames" the text in a criminal

the ubiquity of what he calls the "proprietary model of voice" promotes a crippling dualism between the individual and the social. "One's own" voice is a manifestation of one's own identity: Wordsworth's "man speaking *to men*" (emphasis added) has become today's "speaking subject," whose pronouncements no longer need an audience of the spoken-to to fulfill their function.
67 "All languages . . . are specific points of view on the world, forms for conceptualizing the world in words, specific world views"; "to study the word as such [is] senseless," because it is always "intentional factors," not the "linguistic markers" which linguists study, that identify a language (Mikhail Bakhtin, "Discourse in the Novel" 291-92). "The word in language . . . becomes 'one's own' only when the speaker populates it with his own intention . . . Prior to this moment of appropriation, the word does not exist in a neutral and impersonal language (it is not, after all, out of a dictionary that the speaker gets his words!), but rather it exists in other people's mouths, . . . serving other people's intentions" (Ibid., 293-94).

"Fascinating, ckuhh," the writer murmured. "You have a gift for forceful prose. So when you say that writing is 'framed' you mean that it has an external source, it comes from somewhere else."

"Exactly. They're the same word, 'from' and 'frame': Old English *framian,* to further or advance. That's why you should have your students write 'Dialogue Between the Two Chief World Systems'— nothing is truer to the nature of writing than to get it from somewhere else. Best of all, of course, is to copy something longhand, word for word—the way Shakespeare copied out Ovid and Virgil as a schoolboy, the way the classical Chinese education system worked for centuries. But I'm sure you have your students do that already."

"We most certainly do not. Your originality refutes you," the great writer wiped his glasses and said. "These ideas come from you— anything good comes from the writer's own mind and heart, as I began by saying."

"He's arguing the opposite!" I shouted. "There is no originating self, writing is orphaned, it relies on—"

"On the writings of others? But then those others are originating selves, or 'framers,' and your friend's feelings of absence and non-existence are a purely personal melancholy. Listen," he said kindly to J, "I have students like you all the time. You need to be tricked into doing what you think you hate. The kid who finds Henry James creepy and invasive has the sharpest analytical insight into layers of psychology that I've seen since Henry James himself, but it comes out only when he thinks his characters are describing a landscape. My student who writes the most well thought out, tightly constructed Dickensian plots and subplots thinks she's a loose and spontaneous writer—the structure is secondary but she needs to get it out of the way first, before the important, spontaneous stuff, so she says. You, Sir, are a writer, and a promising one, you just haven't been tricked into it yet. I suggest you apply to our Creative Writing Program. Now," looking ostentatiously at his watch, "if you'll excuse me."

As he stood up and moved us to the door of his office, I tried one last time. "But the tradition—"

"The tradition, ckuhh, what does that mean any more?"

J's subsequent fate, a long, slow slide, can nevertheless be told rather quickly. He abandoned his dissertation: the great writer had convinced him, not that his understanding of the nature of the literary object was flawed but that it made academic criticism impossible. A secondary text presupposes a primary text about which the critic writes, and J no longer believed in such a thing. He no longer seemed to believe in much of anything—perhaps he did not go slightly mad (our mutual friends insist that I exaggerate his mental state), but the sad facts are that semester after semester went by, his teaching ran out, he hung on at the university in one more degrading capacity after another, his clothes grew shabbier, his posture worse.

One day, J turned to me again. "Only who," he misspoke at first, choked with emotion, "only you can write that story. You heard my arguments, you shared them, you must believe them."

"Why bother to write the story if there no longer needs to be a chapter about it?"

"Because I need to rewrite it—instead of writing my dissertation I'm rewriting all the stories my dissertation was about, so I have the same problem now as I had before. You can't copy with nothing to copy." His voice seemed to reach me from a great distance. "Please help me, you have to help me! You have to write 'Dialogue Between the Two Chief World Systems'!"

And so I did.

Acknowledgments

Marshlands, by André Gide

The Custom-House, by Nathaniel Hawthorne

Obasute, by Yasushi Inoue

A Guide to Berlin, by Vladimir Nabokov

Dialogue of the Greater Systems, by Tommaso Landolfi

About the Author

Damion Searls has translated many of Europe's greatest writers, including Proust, Rilke, Robert Walser, Ingeborg Bachmann, Thomas Bernhard, Peter Handke, and Jon Fosse, and he is the editor of a new abridged edition of Thoreau's *Journal*. He has received writing and translating awards from the National Endowment for the Arts, PEN, and the Netherland-America Foundation. His travelogue *Everything You Say Is True* appeared in 2004; this is his first book of fiction. For more, see www.damionsearls.com.

SELECTED DALKEY ARCHIVE PAPERBACKS

FOR A FULL LIST OF PUBLICATIONS, VISIT:
www.dalkeyarchive.com

SELECTED DALKEY ARCHIVE PAPERBACKS

HARRY MATHEWS,
The Case of the Persevering Maltese: Collected Essays.
Cigarettes.
The Conversions.
The Human Country: New and Collected Stories.
The Journalist.
My Life in CIA.
Singular Pleasures.
The Sinking of the Odradek Stadium.
Tlooth.
20 Lines a Day.
ROBERT L. MCLAUGHLIN, ED.,
Innovations: An Anthology of Modern & Contemporary Fiction.
HERMAN MELVILLE, *The Confidence-Man.*
AMANDA MICHALOPOULOU, *I'd Like.*
STEVEN MILLHAUSER, *The Barnum Museum.*
In the Penny Arcade.
RALPH J. MILLS, JR., *Essays on Poetry.*
OLIVE MOORE, *Spleen.*
NICHOLAS MOSLEY, *Accident.*
Assassins.
Catastrophe Practice.
Children of Darkness and Light.
Experience and Religion.
God's Hazard.
The Hesperides Tree.
Hopeful Monsters.
Imago Bird.
Impossible Object.
Inventing God.
Judith.
Look at the Dark.
Natalie Natalia.
Paradoxes of Peace.
Serpent.
Time at War.
The Uses of Slime Mould: Essays of Four Decades.
WARREN MOTTE,
Fables of the Novel: French Fiction since 1990.
Fiction Now: The French Novel in the 21st Century.
Oulipo: A Primer of Potential Literature.
YVES NAVARRE, *Our Share of Time.*
Sweet Tooth.
DOROTHY NELSON, *In Night's City.*
Tar and Feathers.
WILFRIDO D. NOLLEDO, *But for the Lovers.*
FLANN O'BRIEN, *At Swim-Two-Birds.*
At War.
The Best of Myles.
The Dalkey Archive.
Further Cuttings.
The Hard Life.
The Poor Mouth.
The Third Policeman.
CLAUDE OLLIER, *The Mise-en-Scène.*
PATRIK OUŘEDNÍK, *Europeana.*
FERNANDO DEL PASO, *News from the Empire.*
Palinuro of Mexico.
ROBERT PINGET, *The Inquisitory.*
Mahu or The Material.
Trio.
MANUEL PUIG, *Betrayed by Rita Hayworth.*
RAYMOND QUENEAU, *The Last Days.*
Odile.
Pierrot Mon Ami.
Saint Glinglin.
ANN QUIN, *Berg.*
Passages.
Three.
Tripticks.
ISHMAEL REED, *The Free-Lance Pallbearers.*
The Last Days of Louisiana Red.
Reckless Eyeballing.
The Terrible Threes.
The Terrible Twos.
Yellow Back Radio Broke-Down.
JEAN RICARDOU, *Place Names.*
RAINER MARIA RILKE,
The Notebooks of Malte Laurids Brigge.
JULIÁN RÍOS, *Larva: A Midsummer Night's Babel.*
Poundemonium.
AUGUSTO ROA BASTOS, *I the Supreme.*
OLIVIER ROLIN, *Hotel Crystal.*
JACQUES ROUBAUD, *The Form of a City Changes Faster, Alas, Than the Human Heart.*
The Great Fire of London.
Hortense in Exile.
Hortense Is Abducted.
The Loop.
The Plurality of Worlds of Lewis.
The Princess Hoppy.
Some Thing Black.
LEON S. ROUDIEZ, *French Fiction Revisited.*

VEDRANA RUDAN, *Night.*
LYDIE SALVAYRE, *The Company of Ghosts.*
Everyday Life.
The Lecture.
The Power of Flies.
LUIS RAFAEL SÁNCHEZ, *Macho Camacho's Beat.*
SEVERO SARDUY, *Cobra & Maitreya.*
NATHALIE SARRAUTE, *Do You Hear Them?*
Martereau.
The Planetarium.
ARNO SCHMIDT, *Collected Stories.*
Nobodaddy's Children.
CHRISTINE SCHUTT, *Nightwork.*
GAIL SCOTT, *My Paris.*
DAMION SEARLS, *What We Were Doing and Where We Were Going.*
JUNE AKERS SEESE,
Is This What Other Women Feel Too?
What Waiting Really Means.
BERNARD SHARE, *Inish.*
Transit.
AURELIE SHEEHAN, *Jack Kerouac Is Pregnant.*
VIKTOR SHKLOVSKY, *Knight's Move.*
A Sentimental Journey: Memoirs 1917–1922.
Energy of Delusion: A Book on Plot.
Literature and Cinematography.
Theory of Prose.
Third Factory.
Zoo, or Letters Not about Love.
JOSEF ŠKVORECKÝ,
The Engineer of Human Souls.
CLAUDE SIMON, *The Invitation.*
GILBERT SORRENTINO, *Aberration of Starlight.*
Blue Pastoral.
Crystal Vision.
Imaginative Qualities of Actual Things.
Mulligan Stew.
Pack of Lies.
Red the Fiend.
The Sky Changes.
Something Said.
Splendide-Hôtel.
Steelwork.
Under the Shadow.
W. M. SPACKMAN, *The Complete Fiction.*
GERTRUDE STEIN, *Lucy Church Amiably.*
The Making of Americans.
A Novel of Thank You.
PIOTR SZEWC, *Annihilation.*
STEFAN THEMERSON, *Hobson's Island.*
The Mystery of the Sardine.
Tom Harris.
JEAN-PHILIPPE TOUSSAINT, *The Bathroom.*
Camera.
Monsieur.
Television.
DUMITRU TSEPENEAG, *Pigeon Post.*
The Necessary Marriage.
Vain Art of the Fugue.
ESTHER TUSQUETS, *Stranded.*
DUBRAVKA UGRESIC, *Lend Me Your Character.*
Thank You for Not Reading.
MATI UNT, *Brecht at Night*
Diary of a Blood Donor.
Things in the Night.
ÁLVARO URIBE AND OLIVIA SEARS, EDS.,
The Best of Contemporary Mexican Fiction.
ELOY URROZ, *The Obstacles.*
LUISA VALENZUELA, *He Who Searches.*
PAUL VERHAEGHEN, *Omega Minor.*
MARJA-LIISA VARTIO, *The Parson's Widow.*
BORIS VIAN, *Heartsnatcher.*
AUSTRYN WAINHOUSE, *Hedyphagetica.*
PAUL WEST, *Words for a Deaf Daughter & Gala.*
CURTIS WHITE, *America's Magic Mountain.*
The Idea of Home.
Memories of My Father Watching TV.
Monstrous Possibility: An Invitation to Literary Politics.
Requiem.
DIANE WILLIAMS, *Excitability: Selected Stories.*
Romancer Erector.
DOUGLAS WOOLF, *Wall to Wall.*
Ya! & John-Juan.
JAY WRIGHT, *Polynomials and Pollen.*
The Presentable Art of Reading Absence.
PHILIP WYLIE, *Generation of Vipers.*
MARGUERITE YOUNG, *Angel in the Forest.*
Miss MacIntosh, My Darling.
REYOUNG, *Unbabbling.*
ZORAN ŽIVKOVIĆ, *Hidden Camera.*
LOUIS ZUKOFSKY, *Collected Fiction.*
SCOTT ZWIREN, *God Head.*